JUST SOUTH OF SUNRISE

A WILLOW BEACH INN NOVEL (BOOK 3)

GRACE PALMER

JOIN MY MAILING LIST!

Click the link below to join my mailing list and receive updates, freebies, release announcements, and more!

JOIN HERE:

https://readerlinks.com/l/1060002

ALSO BY GRACE PALMER

JUST SOUTH OF SUNRISE
A WILLOW BEACH INN NOVEL (BOOK 3)

It's never too late in life to give love a second chance.

When fate (and a stubborn niece) force fifty-something divorcee Liza Hall to take on a new catering client, the last face she expects to see is Benjamin Boyd.

As in, the very handsome, very familiar Ben who broke her heart many years ago.

That's bad news indeed. Her quiet life in Willow Beach is just what she's been searching for. Why give that up and invite the memory of heartbreak back in?

But it's tough for Liza to resist pressure from her young niece, the pleas of a desperate client, and the man who has always known how to tug on her heartstrings.

And soon, Liza finds herself getting drawn closer and closer to a man she swore off for good.

Can a second shot at love leave her better off than the first?

Fate, family, and food all weave together in this heartwarming second chance romance women's fiction novel from bestselling author Grace Palmer.

Come back to your favorite seaside town, grab a cup of coffee with the Baldwin family at the Willow Beach Inn, and get ready to fall heads over heels for the later-in-life love story you've been craving.

1

Liza surveyed the boxes lining the walls of the storage unit. Hand-me-down dishware, school yearbooks and photo albums, wedding decorations. And above it all, looming over the wedding decorations box like the Ghost of Weddings Past, was a white wicker archway that Liza's mom had insisted she buy for the wedding.

"That's something we can rent," Liza had argued.

"Your children will want to use it at their weddings one day. How can anything be an heirloom if you rent it?"

So, Liza had bought the arch from a company listed in the back of a bridal magazine and then stored it for twenty years, well after her window for having children had slammed shut.

So much for family heirlooms.

No one would want any of this stuff, but Liza couldn't seem to part with it. Even after her now ex-husband Cliff had told her to take or sell or burn whatever she wanted, Liza felt like she had to hold onto some part of their life together. If she didn't, it would all feel like a strange dream. Like twenty years of her life had amounted to nothing at all.

"Ma'am?" The storage facility attendant was a young man, barely twenty, and Liza could tell he was anxious to get back to the lobby and the episode of whatever anime show he'd been watching. She recognized the overdramatic sounds of the anime characters fighting and screaming from when her niece, Angela, stayed with her and tried to introduce her to the genre. Liza never got into the story lines, but it meant a lot to Angela, so she tried.

"Did you want me to take the key from you now, or do you want to drop it off at the front desk?" he asked, impatience covered with a thin veneer of customer service. "If you need more time—"

He glanced around the small space, and it was obvious he couldn't imagine what she'd need more time for. Liza knew the storage unit looked like a pile of garbage to anyone who wasn't her.

"No, I'll be ready in a moment." Liza stepped into the dimly lit room and ran her hands over the faded permanent marker handwriting she recognized as her own, trying to look like there was a purpose to her delay.

There wasn't.

She just wanted to spend one last minute in her old life.

Angela would argue that Liza had already spent far too much of the last few years in her old life. She'd say it was high time to move on. Even though the divorce had been finalized three years earlier, Liza had been in a holding pattern since she'd signed the papers. She'd moved out of the house they'd shared together, but it was only because Cliff was long gone and she couldn't make rent on her own. She had her own bank account, but it was only because Cliff had removed his name from the documents.

Everything that had changed in Liza's life had been done for her. She'd been like a wagon rolling down an incline, being pushed on by gravity, but the moment her wheels hit an obstacle and the slightest effort had been required to push past it, she'd stayed put.

Much like their marriage, the divorce had been Cliff's idea.

In both instances, it seemed like the obvious thing to do. Both times Cliff proposed a change in their relationship status, Liza simply couldn't think of a reason to say no.

～

Cliff took Liza to an Italian restaurant.

He'd just graduated college, so he couldn't afford anything fancy, but the place had candles on every table, free baskets of bread, and a wine to pair with every dish. Even with the plastic red and white checkered tablecloths and cliché Italian instrumental music being pumped through the speakers, it was the nicest restaurant either of them had been to without their parents.

Between the main course and the tiramisu they were going to split, Cliff swallowed the rest of the wine in his glass and then dropped to one knee.

Liza forgot his speech as fast as the words came out of his mouth. Instead of soaking in the moment, she'd been wondering if she could accept. If she should accept.

I don't love him, she thought. But that couldn't be true, could it?

Liza knew how Cliff folded his boxers into thirds in his top dresser drawer. She knew that he hated cheese unless it was melted and that he had two cups of coffee every morning, the first with cream, the second with milk. And she knew that if he was proposing to her, it was because he'd weighed all of the pros and cons and determined this was the best path forward.

With her catering company still in the early stages, she needed someone she could depend on. Liza had already nearly defaulted on a month of rent, but thankfully, she'd picked up an extra birthday party just in time to scrape by. What if that wasn't enough one day? She needed a partner, someone to help carry the load.

At one point, she'd dreamed of romance. Like so many young people, Liza imagined she'd fall in love and the path forward would unfurl before her like a red carpet, leading her into her future.

And then, she lost her job, had her heart broken, and realized that dreams were for sleeping. Life was full of practicalities and problems that needed to be solved. Cliff could solve so many of them for her.

"I love you, Liza," Cliff said, a splash of red across his nervous cheeks. "I think we should get married."

He looked at her expectantly and it was clear Liza was expected to respond to his statement.

In so many ways, it made sense to marry Cliff. But in the one way that truly mattered...

She took a deep breath, shoved that thought deep down, and smiled at him. "I think we should get married, too."

Cliff slid the ring on her finger, kissed her cheek, and sat down as the waiter returned with their dessert. Liza's new fiancé let her have the first bite.

Love didn't wash over people in a single wave. Love at first sight was rare and, in Liza's honest opinion, most likely fake. People weren't destined for one another. Fate didn't play a part in every love story on the planet. For most of history, marriage had been about convenience and security. It was only in the last century that love had anything to do with it.

Even still, love could happen slowly. Like water reaching a boil. Just because the surface of the water was smooth didn't mean things weren't happening below. It didn't mean the water wasn't gaining heat.

It could be still one moment, and then, in one blink, boiling.

Cliff and Liza had been on the stove for a while. Surely, their water would boil soon.

~

The storage facility attendant sighed, and Liza blinked out of her reverie. She swiped her hand across another box and then turned to him and smiled. "I'm all done here."

The kid took her key and hurried back to the lobby. Liza took the back stairs to the parking lot, where Angela was waiting with the now-empty moving truck.

"All squared away?" Angela asked, drumming the wheel.

"I just have to return the van and drop off my apartment key at the leasing office. After that, I'm..."

Ready? Is that what she was about to say? Because Liza didn't feel ready. Far from it. She felt nauseous.

Angela reached across the large bench seat of the moving van and laid a hand on Liza's knee.

"I just need you to remind me why I'm doing this," Liza said, squeezing her eyes shut and shaking her head. "Tell me the plan one more time."

"The plan is twofold," Angela said without hesitation. "For one thing, you need to get away. You need a change of scenery and to meet new people and experience new things."

"I've experienced a lot of new things the last three years," she protested. Liza hated the bitterness in her own voice, but Angela didn't pity her for even a moment.

"You know what I mean," her niece snorted. "Moving into a dinky apartment after selling your house cannot be the height of your excitement for the last few years. The kitchen in that place was microscopic, and the walls were thin enough that you could hear every time your neighbors exhaled. Plus, this trip is going to be good for our business, too."

Liza liked when Angela referred to the catering company as "our business." Even though Angela was still in business school, it was nice to know she was excited about becoming a co-owner of the company. Liza had done well for herself over the years, booking a steady stream of weddings, parties, and banquets, but bringing in a young, passionate partner would only help her brand.

She needed fresh ideas. And Angela had those in spades.

"I wanted you to take a vacation, but seeing as that was impossible," Angela said with a knowing eyebrow raise, "I figured a destination work trip was the only option."

"I've taken vacations." Liza *had* taken vacations, but not since the divorce. Everything felt more manageable when she kept herself busy. Her personal and social life were a hot mess, but the work hadn't changed. Liza liked that.

Angela didn't even dignify Liza's retort with a response. She just kept going as though Liza had never spoken. "It will be great. You'll be house-sitting at this little cottage in this cute seaside town—literally getting paid to water plants and lounge at the beach—and when the relaxation gets too much for your workaholic brain to bear, I've also lined up a wedding for you to cater. It will be perfect."

When Angela had first approached Liza about the plan, Liza shot it down immediately. Moving into someone else's house to cater one small-town wedding? No way. But Liza persisted.

"Heather's aunt is getting married in this cute town called Willow Beach. I looked it up, and it's gorgeous. Like one of those cheesy Christmas movies you like to watch, but with a beach."

"The business is stationed in Boston. I can't take on a client in Maine."

"Yes, you can," Angela argued. "Isn't that why you've asked me to join the business when I graduate? To help you expand."

"Yeah, but I thought you'd help me...I don't know...hire another chef or something."

Angela shook her head. "The two of us can handle the cooking for now, but we're missing out on a lot of weddings by not being more mobile. Plus, your laid-back style of cooking is very well-suited for the beachy wedding crowd. I think it will be a good opportunity."

"I can't move—"

"You don't have to." Angela pulled out her phone and showed Liza a picture of a small cottage surrounded by greenery and rocks and sand. The wooden porch was covered and a hammock hung from two of the posts. "I looked on a few message boards online and found this house. The owner is taking an overseas sabbatical for six months, and she is looking for someone to take care of her house for her. I've got you scheduled to be there for at least a month, rent-free. You just have to pay for food. It's perfect."

Angela had been saying that for the last month. *It's perfect. It will be perfect.* Even now that Liza's apartment was rented out, the storage unit was full, and her bags were packed, nothing about this temporary move to Willow Beach felt perfect.

It felt like a headache.

Angela must have been able to see the stress on her aunt's face because she grabbed Liza's shoulders and twisted her so they were facing one another. "Aunt Liza, you need to get out of this town and get over Uncle Cliff—er—Cliff."

"I *am* over him. It's been three years."

Angela tipped her head to the side. "You might be over him, but you aren't over the relationship. You're holding on to this memory of what you had. You aren't thinking about what you could have. You aren't thinking about the future."

Liza didn't have a good argument for that. Angela was right.

Admitting it didn't feel great, but Liza had been in a holding pattern for years. Somewhere in the back of her mind, she'd deluded herself into thinking this was temporary. As much as she knew it wasn't possible, she couldn't help but think that one day, she'd wake up and everything would go back to the way it had been.

The crazy thing was that Liza didn't even like the way things had been that much. She and Cliff weren't happy. She didn't have a perfect life. It was simply all Liza had ever known, and figuring out a new way to live in her mid-fifties sounded much too hard.

Now, however, Angela wasn't giving her a choice.

"You took a big risk when you started your catering business. This isn't any different."

It's entirely different, Liza wanted to say. This time, she had a choice. But she stayed quiet. Angela knew a lot, but she didn't know everything about Liza's past. There were some things better off being left unsaid.

"It will be perfect," Angela said, not leaving any room for opposing opinions. The moving truck started with a loud rumble. "Fate has big plans for you, Aunt Liza, and I can't wait to see what they are."

It seemed to Liza like *Angela* was the one who had big plans for her, not fate. Either way, she knew her niece well enough to know there was no sense in arguing. So, she buckled up and let Angela lead the way.

2

"This is perfect!"

Angela stood in the center of the small living room, hands on her hips, and a wide smile on her face. Within half an hour, the two women had unpacked all of the belongings Liza had deemed most important—mostly clothes, books, and several boxes of kitchen tools and gadgets—but the next two-and-a-half hours had been spent deep cleaning the cottage. The owner kept a cute house, but based on the stash of pictures Liza had found in the hallway closet and the overpowering stench of mothballs, she was elderly, and the house needed a good airing out.

Angela took down all of the curtains and threw them in the washer while Liza swept and mopped and dusted. The first cold front of fall had set in, so the air coming through the open windows was frosty, but after all the physical labor they'd been doing, it felt nice.

"It's certainly better," Liza admitted. She stood against the wall, still too uncomfortable in a stranger's house to sit down on the sofa, regardless of how exhausted she felt.

Angela crossed the room and bumped her aunt's hip with her own. "Come on. This place is Instagram-worthy. People would eat this up."

"I don't have an Instagram account."

"Which is something else we need to talk about," Angela said, narrowing her eyes and leveling a pointed finger. "We need to build a solid social media presence for the business. People want to see pictures of the food and table displays."

"We have a website."

"Which no one sees. I've seen the traffic, and it's abysmal. We're existing on word of mouth right now, which has worked wonders for you so far. Your organic advertising has gotten us here, but if we want to go further, we need to focus on more pointed advertisement and promotion."

Liza didn't like all of the business talk. She'd left her job in the restaurant industry to start her own business, but she'd never had a mind for it, exactly. She simply made food people wanted to eat at large functions, and that had been enough to avoid advertising and shameless self-promotion and business cards.

But considering even the best reviews on her website included small comments like "She's difficult to get in touch with, but…" and "She's off the grid, but her food is incredible…" Liza recognized Angela's advice was probably for the best. Which is how she'd ended up in this cottage in this strange town in the first place.

"Enough business talk," Liza said, waving a quick hand through the air. "I'll let you handle that side of things, and I'll trust your discretion. Right now, I just want to eat. Are you hungry?"

"Starved!" Angela checked the clock on the wall and groaned, shoulders slouching. "But I have to go. I have to drop off this U-Haul and pick up my rental car, otherwise I'm going to be a zombie in class tomorrow."

"I shouldn't have kept you here as long as I did. I could have cleaned by myself. And now I can't even cook you something. I'm sorry!"

"Don't be. I talked you into this arrangement, so it was only right I come and make sure it wasn't all an elaborate setup to lure you to this beach house and have you murdered." Angela grabbed her purse and jacket from the blue velvet couch and smiled.

Liza arched a brow. "You thought there was a possibility this could be a murder plot?"

Angela shrugged, her blue eyes sparkling in amusement, and Liza could see why everyone thought they were mother and daughter. They had the same curly brown hair and ocean-blue eyes, though Liza thought Angela wore both better.

"Very comforting." Liza couldn't help but laugh and open her arms for a hug. She kissed the top of Angela's head. "Promise me you'll at least pick up something to eat on the road. I left cash in the center console to pay for gas for the truck. Take whatever's left and buy yourself some food."

Angela promised she'd do just that, and Liza waved to her from the porch until the truck was gone. Finally, she was alone.

The cottage looked small from the outside, but there was more room to move around than Liza had expected. Especially in the kitchen.

L-shaped cabinets lined two of the walls with a sizable island in the middle with a butcher-block countertop. It was clear the owner of the cottage liked to cook. Or, at least, *had* liked to cook. Her knives were dull and unsharpened, and most of her appliances were fifteen years old, minimum. The kitchen hadn't been updated in a long time, and Liza was grateful she'd brought so many of her own supplies.

She stopped by the grocery store on her way out of town and picked up a few staple pantry items, some fresh produce, and some frozen meat, so she had the supplies on hand to make her favorite basic shrimp pasta in an avocado-lemon sauce.

Cliff never liked the dish. He complained every time she made anything from the ocean, and claimed the avocado sauce made him nauseous.

Liza stopped making the dish eventually, but since the divorce, she made it at least once a week. The majority of the time, she could convince herself she wasn't bitter or angry with Cliff for blowing up their lives the way he had by bringing their unhappiness to the forefront and calling it what it was, but when she made the shrimp pasta dish, the jig was up. Her bitterness rose to the surface, and this pasta dish he would never know she'd made became her way of getting back at her ex. Her way of sending a cosmic middle finger to him and letting him know he couldn't control what meals she made for dinner anymore.

It didn't matter, of course. He'd never know the difference. Even if Liza called him up and told him about the dish, she knew he wouldn't remember it. Cliff never had a memory for things like that. He was a big-picture guy, not one for the details.

More than anything, though, Liza was bitter that when she cooked, her thoughts were of Cliff.

Before, cooking, whether for work or at home, had been the one time she was able to get out of her head and find joy. Now, she couldn't help but focus on the fact that she was only making enough food for one.

～

Liza sank into the mattress, which was possibly the softest one she'd ever felt. After their trip through the washing machine, the blankets smelled fresh and clean. Still, Liza couldn't fall asleep.

She laid in bed for hours, staring up at the unfamiliar ceiling, wishing sleep would bring a reprieve. But it never did.

Eventually, Liza climbed out of the covers, pulled on a pair of flip-flops with her matching flannel pajama set, and walked out onto the back porch.

The sound of the ocean washing against the shore was muffled inside the house, but outside, Liza could hear it perfectly. It was nature's sound machine, the rhythmic pulse of water reminding you to inhale and exhale.

So many people adored the beach and would talk endlessly about tropical vacations, but Liza never understood the appeal. The sun beating down on you and sand sticking to the sweat. Not to mention crabs and jellyfish and sharks and crowds. No thank you.

This view of the ocean, however, was one Liza had never seen before.

The beach outside the cottage was deserted and quiet. Birds swooped across the sky, black dots on the deep blue horizon, and the moonlight cast the water in a thousand different shades of blue and yellow and white.

Liza could get behind this.

All day—all month, really—Liza had been dreading this move. Her chest had been tight with anxiety that never seemed to ease. On one hand, she knew Angela only had her best interest at heart. She wanted Liza to find her passion for life again, and Liza wanted to find it, too. But it was hard.

For years, she'd made decisions with the single goal of remaining secure. Selling your apartment to house-sit for a stranger was close to the least security she could ever have. Especially since, according to Angela, it carried with it the risk of being murdered.

Now, though, staring out at the water, Liza could breathe.

For the first time in weeks, she felt light.

The wooden stairs groaned under her weight, and she kicked off her flip-flops before she even reached the small gate.

How is this for finding passion? Liza thought. Walking barefoot in the sand under the moon was the kind of romantic, spontaneous thing people wrote inside of cards and used as filler for their bucket lists. It was the kind of thing she'd dreamed about as a young woman; the kind of thing she'd *done* as a young woman before she learned romantic moments didn't always lead to happiness.

Before she learned the true meaning of heartbreak.

Liza took a deep breath of the salty, cool air and shook off the negative thought. Now was not a time to focus on her past. As Angela said, it was time to focus on her future.

Tomorrow, she'd go into Willow Beach and get to know the town where she'd be living for the next month, at least. She'd done some research on the place back in Boston, but she wasn't sure what Angela expected her to do while she was here. The town was mostly a tourist destination, it seemed, which she suspected was the reason Angela sent her here. Even if Liza wanted to work, she wouldn't be able to. The only thing to do was explore the town and relax by the beach. And meet with a client. But one client in a month was hardly what Liza would call work.

As it turned out, thinking about the future didn't exactly fill Liza with a sense of ease, either. She liked to know what to expect, and she liked to stay busy. Here in Willow Beach, she couldn't do either.

A rock outcropping rose out of the sand, a natural barrier that forced Liza to veer closer to the water to get around it. She thought about turning around, but she wasn't quite ready to go stare at the bedroom ceiling again. Besides, with the way her legs were burning from walking through the wet sand, Liza hoped she'd be tired enough to fall right asleep when she did finally go back to the cottage.

Walking through the sand became more of a slog the closer she got to the shoreline, and Liza kept her eyes focused on the ground to make sure she didn't trip over her own feet and face-plant in the sand. With her head down, she didn't see the figure on the sand ahead of her until a foot that was not her own came into view.

Liza jumped back with a surprised yowl, but the wet sand held onto her foot, and she fell on her butt with a squelch.

She expected to look up and see a dead body on the beach. Or, perhaps even worse, the murderer Angela had joked about earlier. Perhaps they'd been waiting on the beach to attack her.

Before she could run either possibility through her mental processors, a pretty woman with curly hair extended a hand to her, face pulled back in an apologetic wince.

"Are you okay? I didn't mean to scare you," she said. "I saw you coming, and I debated saying something, but I thought maybe you'd seen me, and I...I'm sorry."

Liza's heart hammered in her chest, but her fear was quickly shifting to amusement at herself for falling and thinking she was about to be murdered. "Don't be sorry. It's not your fault."

The woman extended her hand again, and Liza accepted, letting her pull her to her feet.

In an upright position, Liza could see the legs of the easel shoved down into the sand with a canvas resting on it. Bottles of paint were scattered on the ground, and the woman still held a palette covered in paint.

"Odd time to paint," Liza blurted more rudely than she intended, brushing sand from her butt.

"It's the only time to paint a moonscape. And I could say the same to you," the woman teased back with a friendly grin. "Most people don't take walks on the beach in the middle of the night. I've been coming out here most nights for the last couple of weeks, and you're the first person I've seen."

Liza told her she was staying at the cottage just down the beach before she realized that might not be the smartest idea. The woman seemed nice enough, but Liza shouldn't be letting strangers know she was staying in a secluded cottage alone.

"Right, Mrs. Albertson's place. I haven't met her yet, but my boyfriend told me she was going out of town. He's the town's mechanic, and she asked him to take her car out for a drive once a week or so to keep it from sitting idle the whole time she's gone." She bent down and started throwing the paint bottles in a tote bag. "She also mentioned she had a woman coming to watch the house, so, I guess that's you."

"That's me. I'm Liza."

"Stella," the woman smiled, pointing at herself with a blue-dipped paintbrush. "Nice to meet you, and sorry to scare you. I'll go a bit further down the beach next time so I don't disturb you on your evening walks."

"I don't walk every night," Liza said. "Or, at least, I don't plan to. I just had a hard time sleeping in an unfamiliar place."

The canvas must have been dry because Stella plucked it off the easel and tucked it under her arm without a second thought. With the other hand, she collapsed the easel and slid it under her other arm. She nodded to the bag on the ground. "Do you mind? I seem to have run out of hands."

Liza picked it up and dropped the handle around Stella's wrist.

"Thank you." Stella paused, truly taking Liza in for the first time. She studied her the way Liza imagined only an artist could, absorbing every detail to the point Liza felt uncomfortable and crossed her arms.

"Well, if you don't manage to get to sleep tonight, you'll be dying for caffeine in the morning, and there's no place better than The Roast. Vivienne makes the best lattes and almond croissants you've ever tasted. It's half the reason I moved here," Stella admitted, her voice low. "Don't tell my boyfriend I said that."

Liza mimed zipping her lips together, and Stella winked.

"Good to meet you, Liza. I'm sure I'll see you around."

Liza waved as Stella disappeared as quickly as she'd appeared, leaving her alone again.

The interaction had been pleasant, but Liza still couldn't shake the uneasiness the surprise had left in her. She'd never been good with surprises, and she didn't want any more tonight. So, she walked back to the cottage at a quick clip, locked the door behind her, and slid back into bed.

Just as she expected, she stared at the ceiling until morning.

3

The Roast was a warm hug of coffee and sweetness. Liza paused in the doorway to fully enjoy the moment. And to take a break. After her sleepless night and her midnight walk on the beach, the walk into town and down Main Street had left her exhausted and in desperate need of caffeine.

"Hi there!" A tall woman behind the counter threw a towel over her shoulder and beckoned Liza inside. She was young—barely older than Angela—but she had a commanding presence. Liza obeyed her order and walked up to the counter. "What can I get you?"

Liza squinted at the menu, cursing herself for not bringing her glasses, and then remembered what Stella said the night before. "A vanilla latte and an almond croissant."

"The latte, I can do," the woman said, spinning around to the espresso machine and talking over her shoulder. "The croissant, however, you're too late for. I'm sold out for the day."

"Darn. A biscotti, then?"

The woman tipped her head towards the display case on the counter, letting Liza know she could serve herself. "If there's anything you need to know about the people in this town, it's that they do not wait around for their pastries. My customers come early and hungry. Especially on a Saturday."

"I'll remember that." Liza used the tongs to grab herself a chocolate chip biscotti and nibbled on the end. It was buttery and crunchy and so delicious Liza felt positive the almond croissant would be to die for. "You're Vivienne, I take it?"

"The one and only." Vivienne spoke loudly to be heard over the sound of the milk frother. Then, with deft hands and a nimble wrist, Vivienne poured steaming milk into the espresso in the shape of a heart. She slid it across the counter to Liza. "And you are...?"

"Liza Hall."

The two women shook hands before Liza gladly wrapped hers around the warm paper cup.

"I don't think I've seen you before," Vivienne said. "There are a lot of people I don't recognize during the summer months, but tourism usually dies down a bit as it gets colder. The beach isn't as fun in a winter coat."

"I'm actually house-sitting at Mrs. Albertson's beach house while she's out of the country."

"Oh right. She's off to the south of France, I think?"

Liza shrugged. "I don't know. I've never met her. My niece actually set all of this up for me. She wanted me to try new things."

"Like living in a stranger's house?" Vivienne grinned, her eyebrows raised.

"Exactly," Liza laughed. "I'll also be doing a bit of work while I'm here. I'm catering a wedding."

Vivienne pressed a hand to her chest. "I had no idea I was serving a bona fide chef."

"From what I've heard of your almond croissants, it sounds like you're the chef."

"Don't flatter me until you've tried one." The bell above the door rang and Vivienne looked around Liza to wave at the new customer before turning back to her. "Come back tomorrow morning, and I'll make sure there is a croissant waiting for you."

Liza thanked her, and Vivienne winked as she started in on the customer's "usual order."

She could have walked back to the beach house or explored Main Street, but Liza's legs were still tired from the walk to the coffee shop. So, she picked a seat in the corner next to a bookshelf full of mass-market paperbacks, board games, and puzzles. She plucked a historical romance off the top shelf and thumbed through it.

How long had it been since Liza had read a book? At least a year, she thought. She used to read all the time. At the end of the day, she'd curl up on the couch in the living room with a blanket and a book while Cliff watched football or worked in the garage.

Liza had deluded herself into thinking the way she and Cliff circled around one another without any need to speak or interact in any meaningful way just meant they were comfortable with each other. Later, of course, she realized they were glorified roommates. And not even roommates who were best friends. They interacted as though they'd found each other through a Craigslist ad and were still waiting on the background check to clear.

Since the divorce, Liza didn't allow herself enough downtime to read. Because, as was currently happening, her thoughts would slide away to the "would've, could've, should'ves," as her mother would have described them. Liza would agonize over where things went wrong. Was it when they decided not to celebrate their ten-year anniversary?

Did their relationship dry up when Liza started spending more time on her business?

None of it mattered, of course. There was nothing left to fix. Even if there had been, Liza didn't want to fix it. Neither did Cliff.

She thought love would come to every couple eventually, if they spent enough time together and worked at it hard enough, but that wasn't true. Some people weren't suited, and after fifteen years, Liza knew she and Cliff were those kinds of people. Still, dwelling on the failure of her marriage left her with a deep sense of ennui that was hard to shake.

She needed a distraction.

"Have you read that book before?"

Liza looked up to see a copper-haired woman close to her age bending forward at the waist to closely examine the front cover of the book she was reading.

"Sorry, dear," the woman said, no doubt seeing the look of surprise on Liza's face. She stood up and waved her hand through the air. "My book club just read that one a few months ago. Actually, I'm fairly certain that is my copy you're holding. Aside from a few of the older gentlemen who frequent the shop, I'm the only one who leaves books here. And I'm certainly the only one who reads romances. The older fellows are into the spy novels."

Liza turned the book around to look at the cover because, frankly, she'd been so lost in her own thoughts she'd forgotten what book she was holding. On the front of the book, a woman in a vibrant pink gown stood on a set of stairs. The dress cascaded down the staircase behind her, and she was looking over her right shoulder, her lips parted seductively.

"The step-back is better than the cover, in my opinion," the woman said, her hand held to the side of her mouth like it was a secret, though she was speaking at normal volume.

The "step-back," as she'd called it, was a sort of secondary piece of cover art on the first page of the book. It showed the same woman from the cover, but the sleeves of the dress were now slipping down around her shoulders, and a man with blond hair in a dark suit held fast to her hand as they ran down the staircase. It was clear, whatever they were running from, they were doing so in a hurry. It certainly made Liza want to read the book and find out what was going on.

While studying the image, Liza noticed a name written in pen on the back side of the cover: Georgia Baldwin. She turned the book around so the woman could see it. "Is this you?"

"Guilty," Georgia said with a kind, confident smile. "I loved the book so much I wanted everyone to read it. I'm afraid you're likely the first person brave enough to pick it up, though."

"Everyone is fine with falling in love and getting married and having kids, but heaven forbid you read a book about it," Liza said. "My ex-husband always made fun of me for reading romance."

"Mine, too. Which is one of the many reasons I'm fine with the 'ex' in his title."

Both women laughed, and Liza felt immediately lighter than she had only a minute earlier. No matter how she described the divorce to people, their reaction was somber and apologetic. Liza didn't want them to throw her a party or anything, but having even one friend who wasn't happily married would have been a solace. Someone who'd understand that, even though there were downsides, there were upsides, too. One of them being that Liza could now indulge her imagination in a romance without her intelligence and taste being questioned.

Cliff would never insult her directly, but he'd roll his eyes whenever she watched the adaptation of *Pride and Prejudice* again. *I'm not sure how much more there could be to take in. They hate each other, they love each other, and then they get married. The end.*

"That one is amazing," Georgia said, pulling out the chair across from Liza. "The author really knows her Regency-era history, and she writes beautifully. I swear, my heart flutters when the two protagonists even brush fingers. It's so romantic."

"I really want to read it, but I'm not sure I'll have the time."

"Take it with you."

Liza glanced towards the counter, her rule-following ways reacting on instinct.

Georgia followed her gaze and laughed. "I donated the book, so I'll clear it with Vivienne if you're worried about it. Besides, like I said, no one aside from the women in my book club ever takes the romance books I leave. I'd rather you have it than let it sit here gathering dust."

It was only a mass-market paperback, after all. Even if Liza did start to feel guilty about it, she could bring it back and buy her own copy of the book for the price of a cup of coffee. "Okay, thanks. I think I will take it."

"Great. You can write your name in right under mine." Georgia smiled, and then her brow creased in a momentary frown. "What name would you write in, anyway? I completely forgot to ask."

"Liza Hall. I'm house-sitting for Mrs. Albertson while she's out of the country." By this point, Liza assumed everyone in the town of Willow Beach knew everyone else's business. They'd likely all know Mrs. Albertson, and at least as far as Georgia was concerned, Liza's theory wasn't wrong.

"Oh, that's right. So you'll be here with us for a while, then? She's supposed to be gone six months, I think?"

"I'm only here for the first month. My niece set up the arrangement," Liza said, explaining her work as a caterer and the wedding she is going to be catering in Willow Beach.

"Does the bride's name happen to be Stacy?"

"I believe so. Do you know her?"

Georgia shook her head. "No, but I run the Willow Beach Inn, and Stacy booked out the entire place for a group of wedding guests."

"Oh, an inn!" Liza said, clapping her hands together. "I've always loved the idea of running an inn. They are so cozy and charming. With what I've seen of this town's Main Street alone, I'm sure your inn is wonderful."

Vivienne called out Georgia's name from behind the counter, and tipped her head to a wrapped-up breakfast sandwich and a cup of coffee. Georgia gave her a thumbs-up and stood up. "Why don't you come see it for yourself? We actually have a book club meeting tomorrow night and it's my turn to host. We're reading a nonfiction book about outer space that Alma picked, but believe me, we are going to spend most of the evening eating snacks and drinking wine."

"I wouldn't want to intrude."

"You wouldn't be," Georgia insisted. "There are seven of us, and we've all known each other for years, so we are well overdue for a new member, no matter how temporary. The ladies are all nice and welcoming, and I swear to you I won't let them badger you with too many questions."

Liza hesitated. She'd never been a social butterfly. While Cliff preferred spending time with their friends and having people over for dinner, Liza liked a quiet evening by herself. All of her favorite hobbies were best done solo, and she wasn't a great conversationalist. Even talking to potential clients filled her stomach with knots.

Still, Angela had pushed her to come to Willow Beach to break out of her rut and try new things. A book club with a group of strangers was definitely a new thing. Plus, Liza felt very confident Georgia Baldwin wasn't dangerous. No murder risk here, that was fairly certain.

"Okay, sure," she said, pushing past her doubts. "Should I bring anything?"

"Only if you want to. I always bring some leftover muffins from the inn's breakfast that day, and Alma is famous for her cowboy Chex mix, but neither of us are professional cooks. I'm sure we'd all love to try whatever you make."

Potential desserts flitted through Liza's mind, the excitement of making something for a group of people that weren't clients momentarily overriding her social anxiety.

"Tomorrow night at seven. To get to the inn, just go east down Main Street, left at the intersection, and follow the winding road until it leads you home."

Liza didn't mean to, but she smirked at Georgia calling her inn Liza's "home," and Georgia caught her.

"That's the whole point of an inn, right? Even if only for one night or a few hours, it's everybody's home." She turned around and grabbed her order from the counter, and then turned back to Liza. "When you see it tomorrow night, you'll know what I mean."

Georgia threw a wave over her shoulder to Vivienne, whose hands were busy washing a coffee pot, so she gave the inn proprietor a smile, and then Georgia tipped her head to Liza and hurried out the door.

Liza watched her go with no small amount of awe. She couldn't remember the last time she'd spoken to a random person in public about anything beyond the long line at the post office or the rising prices of milk, let alone the last time she'd agreed to go do something social with a stranger.

All at once, a memory hit her:

She was waiting tables at the sports bar and grill she worked at, and a dark-haired, green-eyed man kept ordering refills from her even though his glass was still full. When he asked her out at the end of the night, Liza felt helpless to resist. No one had ever spent thirty dollars on soda he didn't plan to drink only to speak with her, and she thought that kind of determination deserved some recognition.

For a moment, her heart fluttered the same way it did that night many years ago. As fast as the feeling came on, Liza pushed it down.

That was a lifetime ago, and this stranger was nothing like the last one. Georgia Baldwin wasn't a green-eyed heartbreaker Liza needed protection from. She was a reader, a fellow divorcee, and a potential friend.

And Willow Beach was a quiet, nice little town. Fully insulated from heartbreak.

4

Angela had arranged for Liza to cater the wedding in Willow Beach, but she didn't have many details. That was unusual for her, being that she was even more detail-oriented than Liza was most of the time, but Liza assumed it was because Angela was more concerned with the move than with the catering event.

It made sense. Liza had catered some of the most high-class functions in Boston. Weddings for heiresses, dinners for CEOs, and charity galas for museums. She could certainly handle a laid-back, small-town wedding.

Still, she wanted to have some ideas to present to the bride and groom at their meeting that evening in case they were the kind of couple who, beyond a few keywords and general vibes for the event, didn't have any direction.

Before she left the coffee shop, Vivienne mentioned the Willow Beach farmers market happening behind the theater, so Liza left The Roast and followed the trickle of women with reusable produce bags to the market.

The weather outside was crisp and dewy with ocean air, but the stalls lining either side of the brick lot provided a modicum of protection from the heat. Plus, almost the moment she walked into the market, an old man in a bright red stocking cap with a long white beard like Santa Claus handed Liza a paper cup of hot chocolate for one dollar.

The drink was a little thinner than Liza liked it, but it was warm and spiced with cinnamon, so she couldn't complain.

Most farmers markets Liza knew of stopped running at the end of the warm summer months, but Willow Beach seemed to adjust with the climate. Rather than fresh flowers, stalls sold square hay bales, cheery orange pumpkins, and apple cider by the barrelful. Summer produce gave way to the deep greens, oranges, and yellows of autumn, and even though Liza had moved with a small refrigerated chest full of her own produce, she couldn't help but pick up a bunch of chicory, a bag of plump grapefruits, and two poinsettias to set on her temporary front porch.

Then, on her way out of the market, an array of beautifully decorated cupcakes caught her eye. A woman bundled in a furry purple coat and matching hat stood behind the cupcakes under a sign that said "Good Stuff Cupcakes." When Liza approached, she grinned.

"Anything I can get for you?" the woman asked. "Or, rather, anything you want to get for yourself? I'm afraid a fuzzy purple coat wasn't the wisest purchase I've ever made. I think I'm shedding."

Sure enough, when Liza looked around the booth, she could see short strands of purple fur all over the ground, which explained why the woman was hiding so far back in the shadows.

Liza assured her she wasn't afraid of a little faux fur, and let the woman surprise her with a cupcake that had candied apple slices across the top and small strips of pastry latticed over top like a mini apple pie. When Liza bit into it, she was met with a gooey caramel center that dripped down her chin, but the cupcake was delicious enough that Liza didn't mind one bit.

"That's incredible," Liza said, not able to hide her shock. "I mean, really amazing. It's the best cupcake I've ever tasted."

"Thank you." The woman looked pleased for a moment before a fluff of purple fur caught a breeze and floated up in front of her face. She frowned and swatted it away.

"Do you do weddings?"

"All the time. Why, are you looking to schedule someone?"

"No, not me. I'm actually catering a wedding in the next few weeks, and I'd be shocked if the bride was able to find anyone able to make a better cake than this. If you aren't already doing her wedding, I thought I'd get your name as a recommendation if she needs one."

"You're too sweet," the woman said. She pointed up to her sign. "I'm Katie, owner and operator of Good Stuff Cupcakes. I'm the premier wedding cake maker in town. What are the couple's names?"

"I don't know any last names, but the bride's name is Stacy."

Katie snapped her fingers. "Yes, I'm scheduled for that one. She wants a rustic, three-tier white cake with fresh flowers on top. Simple, elegant, and, most importantly, easy."

"I know what you mean," Liza laughed. "'Laid-back' is a caterer's favorite word."

"Well, since we'll soon be working together, the cupcake is on me," Katie said.

Liza tried to argue, but Katie waved her away. "Think of it as a thank you for future wedding cake customers you send my way."

Liza didn't know how many people in Boston would be interested in booking a cake company who lived hours away, but if any of her customers ever wanted a small-town ceremony, she'd certainly send them to Willow Beach and Good Stuff Cupcakes.

Loaded down with fresh produce and full of coffee and desserts, Liza hoofed it down Main Street and back to her cottage, her head zinging with new ideas she couldn't wait to try out.

~

Liza always argued she wasn't a superstitious person when Cliff would point out the ritual she performed prior to every first meeting with a client, but now that he was gone and she wasn't so defensive, she had to admit that maybe he had a point there.

It stemmed more from her social anxiety than any actual belief that a certain routine would guarantee her success.

Before each meeting, she made up a simple batch of profiteroles as a gift for the client, took a shower—even if she'd already showered that morning—and wrote down her goals for the meeting and the client-caterer relationship in her planner.

For her meeting with Stacy—last name still to be determined—Liza's goals were simple: find out how many courses Stacy wanted, and try something new.

Even though Liza tried to keep her catering game fresh, it was hard not to have a go-to menu for certain types of events. For instance, she always made roasted tomato and sweet pepper soup with grilled cherry tomatoes for appetizers at autumn weddings. And for gallery openings or museum charity functions, she always made watermelon and feta bruschetta.

She returned to the dishes time and again because they were crowd favorites, but these repeated menus were part of the reason Liza had been in such a funk. Rather than pushing the bounds of her creativity and risking trying something new, she went with the safe option. But Stacy's small-town wedding was already going to be safe enough, so Liza felt like there was room to do something interesting.

After slipping into a simple black dress and curling the ends of her hair, Liza placed eight profiteroles in a small cardboard box, tied it with a ribbon, and then set out for the address of the Italian restaurant Angela had sent her the day before.

It wasn't customary to bring your own dessert into a restaurant, Liza knew, but a little sweet treat went a long way in making a good impression and charming new clients. Besides, they didn't need to eat it at the restaurant, though many clients confided in Liza later that they cracked into the box of goodies in the car on the way home and finished them before they even pulled in the driveway. She wasn't a trained pastry chef, but she knew her way around a profiterole.

Liza had passed Romano's that morning on her walk into town to get coffee. She was grateful it was on the closer side of Main Street to the cottage because, even in her flats, her feet were aching by the time she arrived at the restaurant.

Romano's was a casual Italian restaurant with decades' worth of black and white family photos covering the walls and candles dripping wax in the center of every table. There was one like it in just about every town in America.

But as soon as she walked through the door, Liza was transported to another Italian restaurant years earlier. To a dull-eyed young Cliff offering her a future she wasn't sure she wanted.

Out of habit, she reached her thumb across the inside of her palm and felt the underside of her ring finger where her wedding ring used to be. When she was nervous, she used to spin the ring around her finger. It had taken her almost two years to drop the habit, but it still reared its head every so often.

The hostess was a young woman dressed all in black with her hair slicked back in a tight ponytail. She asked Liza the name of her party, and for a second, Liza nearly gave her Cliff's name. Even when Liza made the reservation, she'd always put it under Cliff's name, knowing he'd be the one to walk up to the hostess stand when they got to the restaurant. She bit her tongue and cleared her throat.

"Liza Hall. It should be a table of three."

"Yes, of course," the hostess said, pointing to a spot Liza couldn't see on her list. "The rest of your party isn't here yet, but I can go ahead and seat you."

Liza could wait outside, but she didn't know who she'd be looking for even if she did. To save everyone the embarrassment, it would be best to take her seat and let the hostess bring the bride and groom to her. So, Liza followed the young woman through the restaurant, weaving between couples leaning over the small tables to whisper to one another and families trying desperately to keep their young children from wiggling out of their seats or throwing spaghetti at their siblings.

Her eyes moved over the rest of the diners in the restaurant, trying to take in as much information as she could about the people, the food, and the atmosphere. If this was the restaurant the couple chose for their consultation meeting, it could mean it was the vibe they were going for in their own wedding. If so, Liza wanted to be prepared.

As she scanned the room, her eyes caught on a head of curly light brown hair in the middle of the room. All she could see was the back of the man, but it was enough to stop her cold in the middle of the walkway.

His hair was long enough that it covered the back of his neck and flipped out over the collar of his shirt. A few corkscrews stuck out at odd angles, familiar enough that Liza was tempted to stick her hand out and work her finger through them.

Cliff had always hated when she did that, but she swore she couldn't help it.

Her heart lurched in her throat, and her stomach fell to her knees, and she blinked at the back of the man's head in utter disbelief.

What was he doing here? It couldn't be.

She was seconds away from taking a step towards him when someone crashed into her back and the sound of glass breaking turned every head in the restaurant.

A waiter had finished clearing a table next to her and backed out from between the tables, only to find Liza frozen in the middle of the walkway. The dirty dishes perched precariously on his tray went crashing to the floor.

But Liza couldn't focus on that. Not while she was still staring at what had—just a second ago, she could swear!—been the head of her ex-husband...

But was now the face of a perfect stranger.

Liza blinked at the man, realizing her mistake. It had all been in her imagination. Cliff wasn't in Willow Beach. Why would he be?

The man frowned, clearly wondering if Liza was having a seizure or an episode of some kind, so, as reality caught up to her, she spun around to the waiter and apologized profusely, her face growing more heated with every second.

"I'm so, so sorry," she pleaded. "Please, let me help clean up."

"It's okay, Ms. Hall," the hostess said as she hurried over, laying a hand on Liza's shoulder. "I'll help Mark with the dishes as soon as I seat you."

Mark, the water in question, looked embarrassed, too, as he stopped down to clean up the mess, even though it had been entirely Liza's fault. To save them both further embarrassment and even more of a scene, Liza apologized quickly again and hurried off to what was, thankfully, a corner table in the restaurant.

"Accidents like that happen at least once a week," the hostess said. "I'm just grateful the glasses were empty. That would have been even more of a mess."

Another memory tickled the back of her mind. She knew better than most that the hostess wasn't lying. Liza was grateful for the woman's attempts to comfort her, but she was even more relieved when the hostess left her alone. She needed to compose herself before her clients arrived—hopefully, well after the glass and shattered dishware had been cleaned up.

Cliff had mentioned something about remaining friends after they signed the divorce papers, but things like that hardly ever work out. It wasn't that they hated one another, but were they supposed to go for coffee or become racquetball partners? Anytime they met, their history would hang over them like a weight, making any activity or conversation difficult.

No, it was easier not to see each other. Though, that carried with it the anxiety that Liza would see Cliff unexpectedly somewhere, and what would she say then?

Hello, nice to see you. Lie.

How have you been? Hopefully not better than she'd been.

Are you seeing anyone? No! The forbidden question. Not to be spoken.

Cliff wasn't in Romano's, but the usual anxiety Liza always felt before a consultation was now amplified by the strange feeling that he would appear at any moment.

It was absurd, of course, so Liza did her best to push the ghosts of her past away and focus on the meeting. She pulled out her planner and set it on the edge of the table. Then, she pulled out her ribbon-tied box of profiteroles and set them on top of the planner, angling them slightly so it looked casual and not as if she'd placed them there just so.

Mark and the hostess made quick work of the spill in the middle of the room, so by the time the hostess was walking towards the table again, two people Liza couldn't quite see walking behind her, Mark had brought the table closest to the accident a free plate of cannolis to make up for the inconvenience and potential danger they'd endured. Liza wondered if she would get a free plate of cannolis, too. Unlikely, since she'd been the one to cause the accident. Plus, then she'd have to explain to Stacy and her husband why she'd been given the dessert, and she wanted to avoid the topic altogether.

The familiar flutter of nerves moved through Liza, and she sat up a bit straighter and resisted the urge to fix her hair. She didn't want to look jittery when her clients arrived.

The hostess smiled at her as she approached, and Liza couldn't help but think there was something condescending in it. A sense of *"don't worry, I won't tell them what you did earlier."* Even though she felt foolish, Liza needed the hostess on her side, and smiled back.

"Here you are," the hostess said, stepping aside with a wave of her arm. Immediately, a middle-aged woman who looked close to Liza's age stepped forward. She had gray-streaked brown hair, laugh lines around her vibrant blue eyes, and a body that spoke to years of a yoga practice or Pilates.

Most of the brides Liza met were young women, wrinkle-free and perfect, just starting out in life. Liza enjoyed being part of their big days, of course, but it made it seem impossible for anyone on the back half of life to find someone. So, this bride was unexpected, but not at all unwelcome.

"You must be Stacy," Liza said, standing up and extending a hand. "I'm Liza Hall. It's wonderful to meet you."

"Liza! Hi!" Stacy spoke with obvious excitement, each of her words punctuated with an octave rise. "It's so wonderful to finally meet you."

"Liza?" Stacy's fiancé stepped out from behind her, and Liza couldn't imagine how he'd ever managed to hide. He was over six feet tall with broad shoulders well-clothed in a cashmere sweater and fitted gray pants.

Liza was so distracted by the sight of him—and horrified by her own indiscretion in perusing his appearance—that she smiled up at him without actually looking at his face. "Yes, that's me. Liza, your caterer."

She moved to sit down, but the man stepped forward and grabbed her wrist, forcing Liza's eyes up to his face.

The moment she saw him—*really saw him*—everything faded away.

Time stopped, the restaurant disappeared, and Liza stared into a face she never thought she'd see again.

The dark hair she'd always admired was speckled through with gray, but it still waved back past his right ear no matter how much gel was in it. Lines fanned out around his eyes and mouth, and his skin was deeply tanned from years of being in the sun. His green eyes, though, were unchanged. They undid Liza just as easily now as they ever had, and she let out a small gasp.

"Benjamin."

He smiled just as he had all those years ago—before she loved him, before he left, before her heart broke—his shoulder lifting in a half shrug. "Just Ben."

Stacy stepped forward with a frown, looking from Liza to Ben. "Do you two know one another?"

Liza's hammering heart jolted to a stop at the realization that she and Ben weren't alone. Someone else was there.

Stacy.

His fiancée.

Ben only smiled and threw his arm around Stacy's shoulders. "Something like that."

5

Thirty Years Earlier

Liza didn't have time to flirt with customers. Men tried often, sauntering up to where she was mixing drinks and leaning against the bar with their hip. They'd exude confidence and ask for a refill and her number in the same breath, as though if they slipped the requests in simultaneously, Liza would give her number to them as part of her job.

"Sorry, no dating customers," she'd say. "Company policy."

There was no such policy, of course. How could there be? Most of the other girls on waitstaff requested their boyfriends come and sit in their sections so they could see them while at work. Still, the lie deterred most men from repeated attempts.

One night, after waiting a table of ten and a drunken bachelor party who spent half of the night screaming at the football game playing on the screen above the bar, Liza didn't have the patience for any more antics. She'd received a meager tip from the large table that did nothing to make up for the headache they'd induced, and after doing her budget the week before and realizing how far she still had to go to afford a year of college on her own, she felt deflated by all of it.

So, when a man sidled up to the bar and crooned a request for her phone number along with a gin and soda, Liza didn't have the patience to even pretend to be nice.

"I'm busy. Ask him," she said, tipping her head to her coworker, John. He was tall and thin, and he gave the appearance that his limbs operated separately from the rest of his body, like a puppet with an inexperienced puppet master at the helm. After a paycheck's worth of broken glasses on his first week on the job, Liza made him swear he'd stop trying fancy bartending tricks and just fill the drink orders.

"I don't want him," the man said, leaning forward so Liza could smell the alcohol on his breath. "I want you."

Liza had a feeling he was talking about more than just wanting a drink, but she ignored him and went about pouring refills for the bachelor party. The groom was already bowled over at the table, too drunk to sit upright, so she'd swapped his drink for a soda. Hopefully he'd be too drunk to notice there was no alcohol in it. For her deception, though, Liza gave him the refill for free.

"Come on." He reached his hand across the bar like he was going to touch her arm, and Liza jerked back out of his reach and fixed him with a glare.

"No, you come on," she spat. "I'm trying to do my job. If you'd like a refill this very second, my coworker is free and happy to take your order. If you're willing to wait, then go sit down at your table and I'll bring it to you when I'm done."

Liza hefted the tray off the counter and lifted it over her shoulder, walking around the bar quickly to try and avoid any more conversation with the flirtatious man. Liza knew he hadn't really done anything to deserve her wrath—he was simply the one unfortunate enough to be there when Liza's tolerance for leering men finally bubbled over—but he also hadn't made her job easier. Rather than listen to her and walk over to John or take a cue from her sour body language, he'd pressed. So, Liza had pressed back.

Still, she felt guilty.

Until she was halfway across the restaurant and heard him behind her.

"I can see that you're stressed, but I think I can help with that. I'll show you a good time."

He dodged a table and lightly jogged to get in front of Liza. His hair was pale blond, almost white, and parted down the center. White fuzz was growing on his upper lip, the beginnings of a very poor mustache, and his eyes were bloodshot.

He was drunk and pushy, and Liza didn't feel guilty at all for what she said next.

"Unless you plan to leave me alone and never speak to me again, I'm not sure what good time you could show me." Liza fixed him with cold eyes for a few seconds, hoping her serious expression would break through his drunken haze. Then, she spun around and walked away faster than she normally would while holding a tray in an effort to shake the man off.

It all seemed to happen in slow motion. Liza was a few steps away when she realized her tray was lighter and slightly off balance. Then, she looked over her shoulder and saw the glasses in the air. Several of them were sideways, liquid already pouring out, and all Liza could do was watch in horror as alcohol and the single soda she'd made for the future groom dumped all over the head of an innocent man.

The incident lasted two seconds, but it felt like hours. Liza stood there in frozen horror as the dark-haired man—even darker now that he was soaking wet—jumped up from his chair and instinctively tried to shake off. His friends all dove out of the way, already laughing at his misfortune, and Liza couldn't breathe.

She'd broken plates in the kitchen, spilled drinks on a table, and even fallen on her butt in the middle of service in front of a restaurant full of people. But never in her years of waitressing had she dumped drinks over someone's head. As she replayed the fall in her mind, she was also fairly certain one of the glasses had hit the guy in the head, as well.

Did he have a concussion? Would she be sued? Would she be fired? Was he going to yell at her?

The man who had been after Liza—who, in all reality, was the reason Liza had spilled the drinks at all—was gone. Either her telling him off had worked, or he'd taken off after her embarrassing moment, likely believing karma had enacted his revenge for him. Either way, he was no longer there to blame, so Liza would have to take full responsibility.

"I'm so sorry," she started, setting the tray down on a nearby table and bending down to pick up the larger shards of glass, as though that might somehow undo the damage she'd done. "This has never happened to me before. I lost control of the tray, and—I'm so sorry."

"It's okay." His voice was deep and warm and, most importantly, kind.

Liza looked up at him and saw he was smiling. And what a smile it was. White teeth with a small dimple in each cheek.

"I was wondering whether I should get another drink or call it a night and head home, and you made the responsible choice for me. Actually, I should be thanking you. You've saved me a real headache in the morning."

He knelt down next to her and dropped a few chunks of glass on the tray, and Liza's heart fluttered. She couldn't smell anything beyond the sickly sweet smell of soda and the bitter alcohol, but she imagined this man would smell amazing. He had on a loose-fitting denim shirt tucked into a pair of tight-fitting denim jeans, and he looked like he'd just strolled out of a catalog.

"You don't have to help," she said quickly. "I should go get a broom and a mop and...find you a towel."

She was flustered and embarrassed and hopeful that she could hide in the back while someone else cleaned up the mess, but before she could get up, the man laid his hand on her arm. "Are you okay?"

Liza choked on a laugh. "I'm the one who dumped an entire tray of drinks on you. I should be asking you that."

"But you're the one who was accosted by a drunk patron, so I'm asking you."

Liza allowed herself to look up at him, pushing past her embarrassment, and she was met with the greenest pair of eyes she'd ever seen. They were green like light filtering through the wide leaves of a sycamore tree—a pale, luminous green. They were mesmerizing. He was mesmerizing.

Liza only realized she hadn't answered when he arched an expectant eyebrow.

"Oh yes. I'm fine," she said. "I'm fine. That happens all the time."

The man chuckled to himself. "So I'm learning. I now understand why you rejected me outright a couple of weeks ago. My lame come-on probably didn't impress you."

Liza was taken aback. If this man had hit on her, she'd remember it. Certainly. He had dark black hair, bright green eyes, and dimples. Liza didn't like being hit on at work, but she had a pulse. She had eyes. She would have taken notice if a guy like this had taken any interest in her.

"You don't remember." He shook his head and smiled shyly, which only made him more attractive. "And you shouldn't. Honestly, I'm glad you don't. It wasn't my best moment. I think I said I didn't need dessert if I had a waitress as sweet as you."

His cheeks flushed, and he squeezed his eyes shut in embarrassment, and Liza couldn't help but laugh.

"See? It was bad," he said.

"I've heard worse."

He cast his eyes up to her, and they caught. For a moment, the mess and the shattered glass and the attention of every single other person in the restaurant faded away, and they were alone. Liza had never felt anything like it. She'd never been so instantly captivated by someone.

"Liza, what's going on?" The sound of her manager's voice broke through her daze, and Liza darted to her feet and spun around.

"I'm sorry, Mr. VanEtton. This was all my fault. I lost control of my tray and—"

"She's being kind to save me the embarrassment." The man, soda still dripping down his neck and soaking into his shirt, held out his hand to her manager. "I'm Ben, and this is all my fault. I accidentally tripped Liza and made this mess. I'm sorry."

Mr. VanEtton comped Ben's meal and dismissed Liza back to the kitchen to clean up and send one of the busboys out to clean the mess. As soon as she had some distance from Ben, she realized her guilt must have clouded her judgment.

He wasn't that handsome, was he? Not any more handsome than any other man who had ever hit on her. She just felt so guilty for drenching him in soda that she wanted to make it up to him. That's what it must have been.

Except, when she came back to the dining room after her break and saw Ben was gone, the disappointment was so sour it turned her stomach.

He *had* been that handsome. And Liza shouldn't have walked away. She should have stayed and asked for his number. He'd apparently already hit on her once. After dumping an entire tray of drinks on him, it was her turn to make the move, and she'd failed.

~

Two days later, when she showed up for the dinner shift after a day off, Liza had mostly been able to push thoughts of Ben out of her mind. He'd been cute, after all, but she hardly knew him. She didn't even know his last name.

Then, she walked to a table in her section and saw him sitting in a booth by himself, his hands folded politely in front of him, an easy smile on his face.

"I'm wearing a windbreaker in case of any unexpected downpour," he teased, smoothing his hand down the water-repellent material.

She narrowed her eyes, but couldn't hide her smile. "I'm surprised you came back at all."

"I was here yesterday, too, but apparently you weren't working."

Her smile grew. "I had the day off."

"We should talk about your schedule ahead of time. I can't afford to pay for endless drinks and appetizers if you aren't going to be the one bringing them to me."

Liza felt like her entire body was buzzing. Who was this man? And how did he have such a strong effect on her?

Liza had dated a few men in the five years since graduating high school, but nothing serious. She didn't have time for serious. She only had time for working and saving money for college. Between working at the photo lab in the mornings and the bar and grill at night, Liza didn't have any time left. So, by all accounts, the warm and fuzzy feeling she felt around Ben was a bad sign for her plans. She needed to keep her distance.

"What can I get you?"

"Whatever you want," he said, handing her the menu without even looking at it. When she raised a brow, he shrugged. "We both know I'm not here for the food, so bring me whatever looks good to you."

Ben came back to the restaurant every night Liza worked, and he always ordered the same thing: "whatever you want."

One time, Liza brought him the most expensive thing on the menu just to see what he'd say. Liza learned he was allergic to shellfish when he didn't touch a thing on the plate, but still, at the end of the night when he walked her to her car in the back of the parking lot, he claimed the time with her was worth every penny.

"What are we doing here?" Liza asked, resting her arms on the top of her driver's side door, one of her legs already in the car. Without other customers and her boss around, she thought it would be best to keep some kind of physical barrier between them. She couldn't trust herself not to draw far too close to him.

Like he always did, Ben shrugged and smiled at her, his dimples on full display. "We're doing whatever you want, Liza."

6

That's it, Liza thought. *I've lost it.*

First, she'd seen Cliff sitting in Romano's, and now, this.

Perhaps one of the plates had slid from Mark's tray and bashed Liza in the head. Maybe that's why she was imagining Benjamin Boyd in front of her after thirty years. Because there wasn't another reasonable explanation.

Unless, of course, he was real.

"Don't keep me in suspense," Stacy said, nudging the man who looked like Ben but couldn't really be Ben in the ribs. "How do you two know one another?"

Liza stared up at the ghost from her past, both cynical and awestruck, hanging on his every word, desperate to hear his answer.

"We're old friends. Liza was a waitress at the bar I liked to go to in college." Ben looked back at Liza and shook his head, his dark eyebrows raised. There were more wrinkles in his forehead now, but those eyes...they were the same luminous green. "It feels like a lifetime ago. I can't believe you're standing here."

That's an understatement, Liza thought. She nodded. "Small world...I guess."

Liza was tempted to turn and run. She'd catered hundreds of weddings. One time, she even catered the wedding of a guy she'd "married" in a playground ceremony on the soccer field in fourth grade. The bride had made a joke about it during the rehearsal dinner, and even though it had been a ridiculous childhood relationship, Liza still felt slightly uncomfortable.

But this? Catering Benjamin Boyd's wedding? Liza couldn't do it. She wouldn't survive. She didn't know if she should warn Stacy to turn tail and run or inform them of her conflicted feelings and leave. The longer they stood around the table looking at one another, however, the more Liza thought she might just collapse into tears.

It had been years since she'd seen Benjamin. Decades. He shouldn't have this effect on her after all that time, but all that time is exactly *why* he had this effect on her. Rather than deal with the messy emotions she had regarding Benjamin and his role in her life, Liza had pushed them down and avoided them. She'd never had a reason to unpack them, so she'd kept them tucked away deep in her subconscious.

Now, without warning, her emotional storage unit had been plundered, and Liza was forced to take stock of every bad feeling she'd ignored for so long. It was a lot, and she wasn't ready.

But she had to be ready.

Liza couldn't afford to fall apart. She had to remain professional for the sake of her business and reputation. But more than that, she couldn't let Benjamin Boyd think, for even a second, that he had any sway over Liza's emotions.

"Well, should we sit?" Liza asked, gesturing back to the table.

Benjamin pulled out Stacy's chair, and she smiled up at him before sitting. Liza slid the box of profiteroles across the table. "I made these for you. A little thank you for asking me to be part of your big day."

Stacy thanked her and then swatted at Ben's hand playfully when he tried to reach for the box. "Mitts off," she warned, eyes narrowed. "It's not your big day; it's mine."

Liza groaned internally. Not only would she have to deal with catering the wedding of an ex, but now she'd have a bridezilla on her hands, as well.

It will be fine, she thought. *I've dealt with worse.*

She was hard-pressed to think of an example worse than her current situation, but regardless, she knew she could get through it.

Liza laughed. "Exactly. It is always the bride's day. I like to sit down with couples, but we all know, when all is said and done, the bride is the one I have to impress."

Stacy lifted a hand towards the sky. "Preach. Yes, exactly. Still, I'm sorry Jonathan couldn't be here. He's the foodie in our relationship."

"Jonathan?" Liza looked from Stacy to Ben, her eyes resting on him for only a moment before she remembered why she'd been avoiding his eyes since they'd sat down. He was far too pretty for a man. It was difficult to look at him.

"My fiancé," Stacy said. "He wanted to be here, but he's out of town on business. He won't be back until just before the wedding, so I asked Ben to come along."

The unsettled feeling returned to Liza's stomach, and she took a deep breath. "Oh. I'm sorry, of course. My niece arranged this, as you know, and she didn't tell me the name of the groom. I only knew your name, so I just assumed—"

"That Ben was my fiancé?" Stacy seemed undecided whether she should gag or laugh. She and Ben both arched away from each other, as though they both smelled something offensive, noses wrinkled. "No, no, no. Not at all."

Ben leaned forward, and Liza wished she'd taken the seat opposite Stacy. As it was, Ben was less than a foot away from her face, and since he wasn't covered in soda and alcohol this time, she could smell the spicy scent of his cologne. It was intoxicating.

He laid his hand on the table, the tip of his finger brushing along the knuckle of her pinkie, and Liza would have sworn he was electrified. A shock seemed to go through her, and she jerked her hand back. Ben noticed the movement, his eyebrow arching in either amusement or offense. Liza couldn't tell because she refused to take in his whole face at once. Instead, she focused on his eyebrows.

"Stacy is my sister," he clarified.

Stacy hummed her confirmation. "He's the bro of honor. Definitely *not* my husband. That would be disgusting."

"And illegal," Ben added. "But mostly disgusting."

The two of them laughed about it, and Liza joined in, but she felt like her body was functioning separately from her mind. Like she was on autopilot while her consciousness hovered above the table, observing everything.

Did Ben have a wedding ring on? No, not that she could see.

Was he married? Was he dating someone?

Would it have mattered either way?

No. *No, no, no.*

It wouldn't. Because this was not thirty years ago. It was in the present. In the now. Liza had come to Willow Beach to get away from her past and focus on the future, and nothing could be more in her past than her relationship with Benjamin Boyd.

~

As far as Liza could tell, she acted professionally throughout the rest of the dinner.

After a few warnings from Stacy, Ben stayed quiet during the conversation about food and the catering style Stacy and Jonathan wanted. Thankfully, Stacy had a lot to say about what she expected. She wasn't a bridezilla, but she definitely had a vision.

She wanted the dinner to be elevated comfort food. "Casual, but classy," she said, shaking her head and laughing at herself. "I know that sounds ridiculous."

"No, I understand what you mean. Instead of pigs in a blanket, we could do chicken sausage and Boursin cheese wrapped in puff pastry. Well, not that exactly, but it's just an example."

"An example I *love*," Stacy said.

Jonathan's family was largely Italian, so Stacy wanted to make sure to honor that part of his history, and even though they'd already hired Katie from Good Stuff Cupcakes to do the cake, they still wanted Liza to make a few small dessert options.

Liza took notes and kept her focus on Stacy, and mostly avoided looking at Ben for any extended period of time except to acknowledge when he spoke to her directly, which was thankfully rare.

At the end of the meal, the waitress came to the table to ask if anyone needed dessert, and Liza shifted her gaze unintentionally to Ben. He was looking at her, too.

Was he remembering the same thing she was?

I don't need dessert with a waitress as sweet as you.

"No, thank you," Stacy said, answering for the table. When the waitress left, she leaned over to Liza and whispered, "I can smell something sugary coming out of the box you gave me, so I'm guessing my dessert is in there."

"You've guessed correctly. Profiteroles," Liza said, wagging her brows.

Stacy clapped her hands and clutched the box even closer to her chest. She held onto it as they stood up and left the restaurant.

Just outside the doors, Ben made as if he was going to say something to Liza or, even worse, pull her in for a hug, but Liza darted away. She pulled her coat closer around her and waved over her shoulder. "It was lovely to meet you, Stacy. I'm so excited to work with you."

"Nice to meet you too! See you soon!"

Liza turned around, but as she did, she heard Ben's deep voice add, "Yes, see you soon, Liza."

~

Stace. That's what Ben always called his sister when Liza knew him. Of course, she knew it must have been short for Stacy, but she'd certainly never expected that Ben's Stacy could be her client. The thought never even crossed her mind.

On the walk back to the cottage, Liza was tempted to call Angela and rant to her about not giving her more details before the meeting, but Angela wouldn't understand Liza's frustration. First, because Liza never wanted extraneous details about clients. Angela handled the details and Liza focused on the food. That was the way they'd come to operate and it worked well for them.

Until it didn't.

If she'd known she was going to be working with Stacy Boyd, Liza would have called off the entire arrangement from the beginning. She'd probably still be in her apartment in Boston at this very moment. Or, more likely, in the small office space she'd been renting out in a commercial building downtown. It cost three times as much as the rent on her apartment, but Liza spent three times as much time there as she did at home, so she figured it all balanced out.

But Liza couldn't explain any of that to Angela because she'd never told Angela about Ben. She'd never spoken a word about him to her because there was no point. He had been out of Liza's life for a few years by the time Angela was born. The two had never met, and Liza never found a good enough reason to bring up a failed relationship from her past. She wasn't still hung up on Ben, after all.

At least, she didn't think so.

Before she could think about what she was doing, Liza pulled out her phone and dialed the first number that came to mind.

"Liza, my dear, how is your new luxurious life at the beach?" Dora asked in a singsong voice she used only when she'd had a few too many glasses of wine. When Angela told Liza her life was boring, the first thing Liza did was point to Dora.

She'd been married for twenty-five years, her youngest son had just left for college, and the moment she came home from work, she slipped into her pajama pants, poured herself a glass of wine, and watched reality television all night long.

"This is just what people my age do," Liza argued.

"What *married* people your age do," Angela countered. "I'm sorry, but unless you want to be single forever, you can't just work and drink wine in your apartment."

Her words stung, but Liza knew she was right. Still, hearing Dora in her natural habitat, happy and content, made Liza wish she'd stayed in her natural habitat, too.

"I just finished dinner at an Italian restaurant."

"That sounds romantic," Dora crooned.

"I was meeting a client."

Dora couldn't hide her disappointment. "More work? I thought this was supposed to be a vacation. Does Angela know you're working on your vacation."

"Angela is the one who set up the meeting." *The meeting with my ex-boyfriend*, Liza wanted to add.

So, why didn't she say it?

She'd called Dora because Dora always knew what to do. Or, at least, she always had an answer. It wasn't always the right answer, but Dora was decisive and confident. For instance, she and her husband had left Boston five years earlier and moved their family to a small farming town in California because Dora decided in the middle of winter that she'd had it with the cold and wanted more sunshine.

So, she moved. As easy as that.

No decision had ever come that easily to Liza.

Which was why she'd sat through an entire dinner with her ex-boyfriend and his sister rather than walk away the way she wanted to. Liza's indecisiveness had kept her glued to that wooden chair in Romano's, and now she'd all but locked herself into a contract with Stacy and her fiancé.

Even if Liza wasn't yet contractually obligated to cater the wedding, it would be cruel to waste Stacy's time only to yank away her services at the last minute because of a long-dead relationship Liza had once had with the bride's brother. Brides hired caterers months in advance. If Liza pulled out, there was a chance no one else would take over.

Besides, it would be childish.

Just like calling her best friend to complain about an ex-boyfriend would be childish. Liza wasn't in her twenties anymore, and she had no desire to go back there.

"You're only taking on the one client, though, right?" Dora asked. "I don't want you going to paradise and then working the whole time. You need to relax."

"I'm not sure many people would call the beaches in Maine paradise."

"You're right. Come to California and experience the beaches here."

Liza laughed, the weight on her shoulders lifting slightly just from hearing Dora's voice. "I can't do that."

"And why not?"

Because I have to cater Benjamin Boyd's sister's wedding.

Liza and Dora had been friends since they both worked together at The Endzone, the same bar where Liza first met Ben.

Dora knew about their relationship and how it ended. She'd spent countless hours listening to Liza talk about Ben, both the good and the bad. More than anyone, she'd understand what a surprise this was.

But also, more than anyone else, talking to Dora about seeing Ben would make it feel real. It would make it feel monumental. And Liza wasn't sure she wanted to give the event that much credit yet.

Really, she and Ben had hardly spoken the entire evening. Liza could feel him looking at her while she talked with Stacy, but neither of them addressed the elephant in the restaurant, and aside from the almost-hug she'd dodged at the end of the night, he hadn't tried anything.

There was a chance she wouldn't even see him again until the wedding. Just because he was the bro of honor didn't mean he'd show up at all of his sister's wedding appointments.

The more Liza thought about it, the more she realized it wasn't even worth mentioning. Telling Dora about Ben being in Willow Beach would only spark Dora's imagination and lead to way too much talk of Ben when what Liza needed to be doing was thinking about Stacy's catering menu and relaxing.

"Hello?" Dora asked. "Is this long pause because you're trying to think of a reason why you can't come visit your best friend in Cali? If so, please stop and just book a flight."

"I can't because I've agreed to house-sit this beach cottage for at least a month. And, like I said, I have a wedding to cater."

"Pssh." Liza could imagine Dora screwing up her face and waving her hand in the air, her wine sloshing dangerously up the sides of her glass. "If you're not coming to see me, then to what do I owe this late-night phone call?"

Liza rolled the possibility over in her mind once again, and decided, finally and firmly, to lie through her teeth.

"I needed to hear my best friend's voice," Liza said. "I miss you. I don't know very many people in this town yet, so I'm all alone here."

"Awwww, sweetie. That's so nice. I miss you too. You know I do. Always."

Liza smiled. "I know. And I promise, once things calm down, I'll finally come for a visit."

"Yeah, right. We both know that will never happen. Whether it's your personal life or work, you're always putting out one fire or another."

"Not this time," Liza said, pushing thoughts of a green-eyed silver fox out of her mind. "Everything is going to calm down soon, and I'll make the trip. Just you wait."

7

"The reunion after so many years, the way he wanted to hug her but held back, the romantic *tension*. It was almost too much to handle."

Liza thought the book club would help her forget about her run-in with Benjamin Boyd, but clearly, the book everyone had been reading was just a fictionalized version of her life. From what Liza could tell from Gwen's brief run-through of the plot, the hero and heroine met when they were in their mid-twenties, but after almost a year together, fate ripped them apart only to reunite them decades later.

"Second-chance romance," Gwen said, tucking a strand of curly gray hair behind her ear. "It's my favorite romance trope. Seeing the characters come together again and then dance around each other, both trying to delay the inevitable—it's so romantic."

Liza wasn't convinced.

Georgia waved her arm to stop the chatter. "Let's not ruin the whole book for Liza. She hasn't read it yet."

"It ends in happily ever after," Alma said, her Texas drawl thicker than it had been when Liza had first arrived. It seemed wine brought out her accent. "Like every romance novel in existence. *Surprise!*"

Georgia elbowed Alma in the side, but the trio of women who had all arrived together—Barb, Pam, and Cheri—started talking at the same time, each of them trying to explain that romance novels were much more than their happily-ever-afters. *They're about the journey.*

Liza had only known most of these women for half an hour—save for Georgia and Stella, whom she'd known for closer to forty-five minutes including their initial meetings—but she could tell she liked them all already. She liked the dynamic they had as a group. Everyone seemed to bring their own energy and personality, but they complemented one another well.

Alma, by all accounts, was the tough cynic. She was loud, opinionated, and did not give in easily to other's persuasion.

Gwen was Alma's opposite. Soft-spoken, sensitive, and starry-eyed.

Georgia fell somewhere in the middle, and Liza could relate to that. She seemed to *want* to view the world through rose-colored glasses, but much like Liza, life and romance had not been the kindest to Georgia. Going through a divorce can damage your belief in happily-ever-afters.

"Are we going to talk about the book or should I start uncovering the snacks?" Stella asked, trying to break through the din of voices.

Stella made the plans. She was organized and structured, and she liked to be in control. Liza could relate to that, too.

"I've already eaten a bowl and a half of Liza's homemade Chex mix," Pam said, laughing and burying her face behind her hand so all Liza could see was the gray streak at the front of her hair. "I'm sorry, but it's so good."

Cheri and Barb laughed and held up their own bowls.

"You sneaks!" Stella yelled, trying to hide her laugh. She shook her head and waved everyone on. "Fine. Eat your snacks, you barbarians."

The Lion King had been Angela's favorite movie as a kid, and Cheri, Barb, and Pam reminded Liza of the hyenas. Not that they were dumb, of course, but they seemed to exist purely to have fun, egging one another on. They laughed at each other's jokes, and if one of them got into trouble, Liza felt confident all three of them would be there to help.

Everyone had a place within the group, a role that they held and tended. Liza wondered what hers would be.

It didn't matter, of course, because she wouldn't be in Willow Beach long, but still, she wondered.

"These cookies are devastatingly good, Liza." Stella stacked two on her plate and wrapped one in a napkin. For later, Liza assumed.

"I call them leftover cookies."

"Left over from what? Who would possibly leave any of these behind?" Alma asked.

"They don't. That's why I call them that," Liza laughed. "There are never any left over. And I make them with a lot of leftover baking ingredients—chocolate chips, caramel chips, toffee. They change a little bit each time I make them, but they're always a hit."

The women were being nice to Liza about her snacks—probably because it was her first time at the book club and because, not to be braggy, Liza was a good cook—but Liza liked everything everyone else had brought, too.

Alma had made what she called "cowboy caviar," which was a mix between seven-layer dip and a corn salsa, and she had also brought homemade tortilla chips. Georgia presented leftover blueberry lemon muffins from the inn's breakfast that morning, but they were so fluffy and flavorful that Liza was certain they would be her favorite muffins ever when fresh. And Stella brought a bag of cannolis from Romano's.

"I never would have refused dessert last night at Romano's if I'd known this is what I was missing out on," Liza said. The golden brown shell was crisp, and the creamy filling inside tasted sweet and bright and balanced in a way many decadent desserts aren't. Whoever made the cannolis at Romano's knew what they were doing.

Stella held up a cannoli and examined it with obvious admiration. "Sometimes I make Sam take me there just for cannolis. We skip real food and go straight for these and espresso. They are addicting."

After a while, the book was set aside in favor of food and conversation, and Liza liked how easily she fit in here. She knew everyone was treating her especially nicely since they'd just met, but she could also tell none of these women were fake. Their niceness wasn't forced. They were genuinely good people.

"So, Liza," Cheri said, dabbing her lips with a napkin before she continued. "Word on the street is you are catering a big, fancy wedding here soon. Someone thought you might have been brought here from Boston exclusively to cater the wedding, in fact?"

"That 'someone' she is referring to is herself," Pam fake whispered, nudging Cheri in the side.

Cheri blushed slightly and shrugged, not denying the claim.

"No, not at all," Liza said. "Well, it's true I'm catering a wedding, but it isn't a fancy affair, just a big one. The bride said the groom is the youngest of ten kids, so his family is large. And I'm here to house-sit Mrs. Albertson's beach house while she is out of the country. It just so happens that my business partner found some work to keep me busy, too."

"Ten kids?" Georgia blanched. "I'd die. Three is more than enough for me."

"Speaking of your kids…" Alma lifted her chin and pointed her wineglass towards the stairs as two young women mounted them.

One of them had dark, curly hair and an angular face, and the other was a younger version of Georgia. She had the same coppery hair and bright smile. It was uncanny.

"Are we interrupting?" the younger Georgia asked.

"Never!" Georgia said, standing up and throwing her arms wide. "We were just talking about you two."

The woman who looked identical to Georgia was Melanie, Willow Beach's resident veterinarian, and the darker-haired woman was Tasha, the family's actress.

"Tasha and her boyfriend hosted an improv class for my guests earlier this evening." Georgia seemed proud of this offering, but Liza could think of nothing more unbearable than attending an improv class. Just the thought gave her hives.

Tasha wrinkled her nose. "Yeah, that's going to be a one-time thing, Mom. Nobody liked it. The handsome man staying in room five tried to act enthused, but he was just being kind. Improv is not for the unsuspecting masses."

Georgia waved a hand. "They don't know what they're missing. You and Eddie did great. You make a wonderful team."

Tasha groaned. "If you hint at marriage one more time, Mom, I'm going to swear off the institution altogether."

"No one's pressuring anyone." Georgia lifted her hands in surrender. "I just know a good thing when I see it, and I hope you do, too."

Tasha rolled her eyes and nudged her sister. "Melanie, tell everyone about Colin and make Mom stop talking about me."

Melanie's eyes went wide. "He's fine. We're fine. Let's talk about something else."

"No, no, no." Georgia stood up and pushed her daughters towards the stairs, talking over her shoulder as she went. "I swore I'd never be the mother who embarrassed her daughters—"

"Too late," Tasha laughed.

Georgia ignored her. "Let's walk on the beach and let some of the ocean air chase away the wine fog."

No one needed any encouragement. The autumn sun was already setting low over the water, casting the waves in shades of orange, purple, and blue. It was lovely.

Liza liked the city. She liked walking out her front door and being half a block from a bakery, an ATM, and a gym. But there was something to life on the beach, too.

Every time Liza looked out on the ocean, she felt a calm unlike anything else wash over her. Like she somehow became the ocean, swaying with the wind and the current. Like she didn't need to strive one way or the other. She simply needed to *be*. It was a feeling she'd experienced only a few other times in her life.

Long-ago memories of Benjamin threatened to crest the surface of Liza's peacefulness, and she swatted them away. She was only thinking about him because she'd seen him last night.

"Peaceful, isn't it?"

Liza turned and saw Stella walking towards her. The rest of the book club was cooing over something that was scuttling across the sand—a crab, Liza thought.

"I've never been one for the outdoors. I'm *indoorsy*, as Sam likes to say, but even I can't turn down a walk along the beach for this kind of view. It's beautiful."

"It is," Liza agreed. "I was just thinking the same thing. I've always lived in a city, so I don't have a lot of experience with nature, but this is great. Calming."

"When your month at Mrs. Albertson's is up, Boston will feel like chaos to you. At least, that's what it felt like for me when I had to go home and pack up my stuff before moving here."

"Did you live in Boston, too?"

"No. It was a small town compared to most towns, but it's a metropolis compared to Willow Beach. This place is special." Stella looked over at the women who were now crouched down and waddling along after the crab as it made its way to the ocean. Liza had a feeling she was talking about more than the scenery. "I get to walk wherever I want, I've made more new friends than I ever expected to at my age, and I found love."

"Isn't that wild?" Liza mused. Stella raised her brows curiously at Liza's comment, so she continued. "I don't think the two of us are old. We're on the back half of life, but just barely. Yet, the world trains us to think life is over. Making new friends? That's a young person's game. Finding love? No way, too old. But I don't feel old."

"I don't anymore," Stella said. "I used to, though. My son went off to college, and I was ready to buy some stretchy pants, trade in my heels for orthopedic shoes, and dye my hair blue."

"Blue wouldn't be a good look on you. No offense."

"None taken." Stella shrugged. "I just wasn't sure what my purpose was after my son left, you know?"

"I don't have kids, so not really, but I remember how weird it was sending my niece to college. I was convinced I'd never see her again."

"But now she's your business partner? Did I hear that right?"

"You did. She's going to help me run my catering business. Her going off to college was amazing. After a year of not knowing what she'd do, she went into business and then emailed me her proposal to run things, and now I'm not sure where I'd be without her. Especially after my divorce, I was lost. Work is the only thing that kept me going, and Angela is the only reason I had work to do. She scheduled all of our clients for months."

Stella frowned. "Were you married for a long time?"

"Twenty years."

Stella winced, and Liza nodded. "Yeah, it's not the way I thought things would end up. But then again, I also feel like it was for the best."

"You're happier now?"

Liza had avoided asking herself that question because she knew the truth, but now, there was nowhere to hide. Stella was a nice woman. Liza could tell that, even though they'd only just met, she wasn't asking her these questions out of a sick kind of enjoyment. She genuinely wanted to know.

So, Liza told her. "I'm not. But, eventually, I know I could be. That's part of the reason I'm here in Willow Beach."

Stella smiled and laid a hand on Liza's shoulder. "I hope you find it."

The crab had finally made its way to the water, and the rest of the ladies were walking towards where Stella and Liza were standing on the beach, laughing and joking with one another. Liza didn't know any of them well, but she had a feeling they all knew a thing or two about being happy. Liza decided then and there that she'd be open to whatever this town and its people had to teach her. She wouldn't let this trip and all of Angela's hard work go to waste.

8

Liza was trying to be open-minded about finding happiness in Willow Beach, but she was fairly certain that even the most open of minds couldn't find any reason to be happy about a burst water pipe.

She got up a few hours after going to sleep to use the restroom, but as soon as she opened the bedroom door she stepped in a puddle. The water was coming from the bathroom, and it didn't take a certified plumber to know a pipe had burst.

Liza spent twenty minutes fumbling around the house in her now soggy pajama bottoms, trying to figure out how to turn the water off, and then another twenty minutes trying to get in touch with Willow Beach's only plumber before she decided to jump ship. She unplugged everything within the danger zone, grabbed her luggage, and called a ride share to take her to the Willow Beach Inn.

Everyone was asleep when she arrived, but the bell next to the front door brought Georgia down in her pajamas and a robe, a sleepy smile on her face.

"Hi there, how can I—Liza?" Georgia took in the sight of Liza in her wet pajama pants and her luggage and frowned. "What are you doing here, darling? Here, here, come in." Georgia ushered Liza inside and into the dining area.

The inn was adorable, just like Liza expected. It had the old-world character people wanted in an inn—original woodwork, intricate tile floors, and large chandeliers hanging from high ceilings. Still, even with all of the finery, it had a cozy feeling. Like home.

"Not that I'm not happy to see you at midnight, but what are you doing here exactly?" Georgia asked again.

"A water leak." Liza was much more tired than she thought, and describing the situation she'd been dealing with for the last hour felt taxing. "A leak in the bathroom, I think. A pipe burst. I'm not sure, but I woke up, there was water everywhere, and I couldn't figure out how to turn it off. I called a plumber, but—"

"Oh, Jack won't answer until the morning. For late-night plumbing issues, you're on your own unless you knock on his door. But even then, he's pretty surly." Georgia bit her lip, thinking, and then snapped her fingers. "Drew and Joel do a lot of maintenance around here. Let me wake them up."

"No, please don't. I just came here for a place to sleep," Liza said.

Georgia started towards the stairs. "Nonsense, dear. We can't let Mrs. Albertson's house go the way of the ocean. We need to get your water turned off as soon as possible. They'd be happy to help."

Liza stood for a minute, unsure what to do, but eventually, exhaustion got the best of her and she dropped down into one of the chairs at the dining tables. If Georgia wanted to wake people up to help, she wouldn't stop her. God knew Liza could use assistance.

Cliff had handled all the maintenance around their house. Liza could use some basic tools and did her fair share of painting and light remodeling, but she'd never touched a water shut-off valve in her life. She had no idea what to do when something seriously went wrong because she'd never needed to know.

Until now.

Liza heard voices and stood up just as Georgia turned the corner, smiling and talking with someone behind her.

"You really don't need to do this. I can go wake my son up. And I'm sorry we woke you up."

"It's fine," a male voice said.

A very, very familiar male voice.

Liza had the urge to squeeze her eyes closed and try to wake up because, surely, this was a bad dream.

But, no. Georgia walked towards Liza, her eyes wide and eyebrows raised like she had a big surprise hidden behind her back, and she did. But Liza wasn't happy about it.

Benjamin Boyd followed Georgia into the dining room.

"I couldn't sleep anyway. I'm a bit of a night owl," he said to Georgia. "Plus, I've done a bit of everything. I worked as a campus handyman for a year after high school. Well, I was more of an assistant to the campus handyman, but I dealt with my fair share of plumbing issues."

"Hear that, Liza? I found you a bona fide plumber right here in the inn. Isn't that great?" Georgia smiled up at Ben with the soft eyes he'd probably been getting from women his entire life. Liza knew Georgia was happily in a relationship, but that did little to dull the effect of Ben's square jaw, broad shoulders, and overall maleness.

Generations of instincts required every woman in the vicinity to turn to jelly in his presence.

Liza refused to give in so easily, though.

"I don't need a plumber. The leak is very small. It can wait until Jack is awake. I just need a place to sleep tonight, and then I'll call first thing in the morning."

Ben turned his head to the side, his green eyes bright even in the dim light. "If it's only a small leak, why do you need a place to sleep tonight?"

Liza narrowed her eyes at him and ground her teeth. "Out of an abundance of caution."

"Well, out of that same abundance of caution, how about I go help you at least turn off the water and drain the pipes? That will keep things from getting worse."

Georgia's brow furrowed, no doubt sensing the tension between Liza and Ben. "I tried to tell Mr. Boyd that he didn't need to help, but once he knew what was going on, he insisted."

"It's the least I can do for the caterer of my sister's wedding." Ben smiled at Georgia and then turned back to Liza, one eyebrow arched. "Shall we? I saw a driver drop you off earlier, so I can give you a ride if you don't have a car. My rental is parked out back."

So, he had known it was Liza who needed the help. Benjamin wasn't some gallant knight, swooping in to rescue just any damsel in distress. He knew Liza was downstairs, and he'd intercepted Georgia to insert himself into the mix.

What benefit he hoped to get out of the arrangement, Liza didn't know. It wasn't her house. Whatever the repairs cost would be coming out of Mrs. Albertson's budget.

Georgia gave Liza a nervous look, and Liza smiled as casually as she could.

"Yes, I'm ready. Let's go."

$\sim$

Mistake.

Liza had made a grade-A, top-notch, code red mistake.

To be fair, she hadn't been in a car with Benjamin Boyd in over two decades, so she'd forgotten how much more potent his allure could be in close quarters.

He smelled spicy and warm like mulled wine and cedar chips and lemon wedges, and Liza had the sudden urge to stick her head out the window like a dog.

Thankfully, the drive to the beach house was short, and aside from asking Liza a few questions about the extent of the leak, Benjamin didn't try to make conversation. Liza didn't know what they'd talk about if he did.

Long time no see. What have you been up to the last twenty-five years?

With horror, Liza realized she couldn't talk about the last twenty-five years. Because if she did, she'd have to tell Ben she was now divorced.

She didn't want him to think, for even a second, that her life had turned out any differently because of him and what he'd done. She didn't want him to wonder if her divorce was because she couldn't love Cliff the way she'd loved Ben, or if he had somehow factored into her decision to not have children.

Of course, at the same time, Liza was desperate to know if Ben's life had been any different since their uncoupling.

Did he get married? Have kids? Had his life been happy?

"Were the rest of your clothes ruined when the pipes burst?" Ben closed the door and looked at her over the top of the rental car, his mouth twisted into a knot—his failed attempt at hiding his amusement at her damp flannel pajama bottoms.

He'd teased her all the time while they were dating. At the beginning, he'd been all smoldering eyes and kind words, but as they got to know one another, Benjamin liked to get under her skin.

"You look adorable when you're annoyed with me," he used to say.

"Then I must look adorable all the time," she'd quip back.

Liza sighed, doing her best not to look annoyed, though she felt it immensely.

"No, I just didn't see a point in changing my clothes just to change back into pajamas at the inn. Like I said, I wasn't there to secure the help of a plumber. I was there to go to sleep."

"Well, it's your lucky day, then." He turned towards the house. "I'm going to assume you've been downplaying the situation, and I'm about to walk into a tsunami. Is that true?"

"No, of course not. Why would I—"

"Liza," he said, lowering his chin and raising his brows. "Give it to me straight."

Liza wanted to lie, but there was no sense in it. He'd know she was lying the moment he walked into the house. It was just that Liza didn't want Ben to know anything about her. They hadn't seen each other in decades, so he shouldn't know she had a tendency to downplay situations to keep other people calm. He shouldn't know that she hated asking for help, so she'd lie and say things were fine even as they were falling apart.

She mumbled something, and Ben held a hand to his ear. "What was that?"

"Yes!" she barked. "It's a tsunami inside."

He chuckled as he walked towards the porch, which was worse than anything he could have said. It sparked something inside of Liza that had been dormant for a long time.

She gripped her keys in her hand and stomped after him, brushing past him to get to the front door so she could unlock it. She had to fight back a shiver, both from the cold on her wet legs and Ben's presence.

"I lied because I didn't want *you* to help," she said between gritted teeth. "I lied because I went to the inn for a place to sleep, not to find an ex-boyfriend to drive me home and come fix all of my problems. I can probably fix it myself, in fact. I barely even tried."

"That's good, because that would have been a very specific request. I can't imagine you have many ex-boyfriends wandering around in this small town. Or, maybe I'm wrong," Ben said with an easy shrug. "I suppose I don't know what you've been up to the last twenty-five years. Maybe this isn't your first time in Willow Beach."

Liza got the door unlocked and spun around to gape at Ben's forwardness, but before she could, he walked into the house and flipped on the lights.

Liza was still ready to rant at him, her blood pressure dangerously high, but Ben cursed under his breath and splashed down the hallway and away from her anger.

The water shut-off valve was in the garage, somewhere Liza never would have thought to look. Ben shut it off and then directed Liza to start turning on faucets and flushing toilets.

"That seems counterproductive."

"We have to drain the pipes," he said. "It's better the water comes out into the sink than through the hole in your bathroom wall."

Liza had been too distracted by the gushing water to realize there was a hole in the wall. A large one.

More and more, it seemed coming to Willow Beach had been a mistake. Sure, she'd discovered a love of the ocean. But Liza had also reunited with a man she'd hoped to never see again and had to trek all over town in dirty, soggy pajama pants because of a leak.

None of this would have happened in her apartment in Boston.

Liza would have called the twenty-four hour maintenance staff and had someone sent up right away to take care of the problem. She would have stayed dry and far, far away from wherever it was in the world Benjamin Boyd called home.

The sinks were all finally empty when Ben jogged outside and returned wheeling a wet/dry vacuum across the living room.

"Do you always keep one of those in your car?"

"I grabbed it from the maintenance closet at the inn before we left. I thought we might need it, knowing your penchant for downplaying tragedy." He plugged it in and winked at her as he began vacuuming up the water.

Liza shouldn't be mad at him. It was after one in the morning, and Ben was here, stopping leaks and cleaning up. By all accounts, it was a nice thing to do, and Liza should be thanking him. But she couldn't.

Ben dumped the vacuum outside several times before most of the water was gone from the hallway. When he came back in the fourth time, he left the vacuum outside. "I think that's as much as the vacuum can do, but I'd say it's a good start."

"Not bad," Liza said, crossing her arms and studying the hallway with laser focus. Anything to keep from looking at him.

"I know you weren't asking for my help, but I hope I've helped you out a bit." He was fishing, and Liza knew it. She resisted.

"Yep, you have."

"This might have taken you all night if not for me," he continued.

She turned away and rolled her eyes. "Actually, it would have taken me all morning. I'd be asleep right now if it weren't for you."

"And the cottage would be underwater."

Liza bit her lip. How did Ben still know how to get under her skin? It wasn't fair.

He chuckled. "It's okay. I know asking for help isn't one of your strengths, of which there are many, by the way. I'm glad to see you followed your dreams and started your own business."

The topic change came on suddenly, and Liza couldn't help but turn towards him in an attempt to find her bearings. Was he still teasing her or was his compliment genuine?

Mistake.

There was a sheen of sweat across Ben's forehead and color in his cheeks that only added to his natural appeal. In his hurry to come help her, he'd left the inn wearing a pair of gray jogger sweatpants and a thermal long-sleeved shirt that clung to his body. Time had peppered his hair with gray and creased his face, but he was still broad and muscled.

Liza jerked her eyes up to his face and met his confident, yet sincere smile. His green eyes crinkled at the corners.

"Thanks," Liza mumbled, finally able to say the word, but only in regard to her business. Because she was proud of the company she'd created and the job she'd made for herself. She could thank someone for recognizing her success, no matter who they were.

"Really," Ben continued, his brow becoming pensive. "You always talked about wanting to do more and make your own future, and you did it. That's amazing. After we parted ways, I wondered what happened to you. I looked you up a few times and—"

"Can we not?"

Liza felt like her chest was being squeezed in a vise, like she couldn't expand her lungs far enough to take in air.

Seeing Ben was one thing, but talking about their past? Their relationship? No way. She couldn't do it. She didn't want to. The book had closed on that chapter of her life, and she was all about forward progress. No looking back.

His mouth opened and closed, unsure. "I'm sorry. I just—"

"I'm glad you're doing well," Liza said, despite having no basis for whether Ben was doing well or not. He looked well, and she hoped that was enough of an indicator of how he was doing in other areas of his life. At the very least, she could tell he had enough to eat, enough time to work out, and enough money to pay for regular haircuts and dental appointments. So, he was probably doing fairly well.

"I really am," she continued. "But I don't want to talk to you. We can see each other at your sister's wedding, and then I think it would be best if our paths didn't cross again."

Obvious hurt crossed Ben's face, but Liza couldn't focus on that. She had to do what was right for her, and she and Angela had both agreed—mostly Angela, in truth, but Liza was coming around to the idea, as well—that she needed to focus on her future.

Ben was, inarguably and decidedly, in her past.

After a long pause, Ben nodded and tipped his head towards the door. "I suppose I should go."

Liza nodded and crossed her arms, giving him a tight smile.

She shut the door as soon as he walked through it, and she stood by the door until she heard the car start and saw the headlights flood through the windows of the cottage and then fade away.

Only then did she relax and begin to take stock of the damage in the cottage, avoiding thoughts of Ben all the while.

9

Liza called Jack first thing in the morning. She quickly discovered that Georgia was right; the man was surly.

But since he fixed the pipes and allowed Liza to take a shower for the first time in thirty-six hours, Liza decided he could be as surly as he wanted.

Mrs. Albertson had a stash of money set aside for just such an emergency, so Liza paid Jack with that money and then took a long, hot shower.

There was still a hole in the bathroom wall courtesy of who-knows how many months and years of a steady leak behind the wallpaper, and water stains in the hallway. But the bulk of the problem was fixed, and Liza felt like she'd done her duty as a house sitter to the best of her abilities.

Still, the preceding days had been a whirlwind of excitement and nostalgia, both good and bad. Liza felt drained. She considered going into town for lunch, but worried about running into Ben again, so she opted for pizza delivery instead.

"Pizza and boxed wine. Living the dream," she mumbled, raising her mason jar in a solo toast before digging into her meal.

Afterwards, she slipped out of her shoes and went for another walk on the beach.

The weather seemed to be getting colder by the day, and the sand felt like sharp pinpricks in the soles of her feet, but that didn't do anything to lessen the relief she felt to be standing out in the open and hearing the rush of the waves. Suddenly, Liza could understand why people enjoyed meditating.

"We meet again."

Liza started at the voice, but relaxed as soon as she turned and saw Stella waving. She had an easel set up in front of her, and was nestled back in a beach chair, a fuzzy blanket wrapped around her shoulders.

"Still working on your moonscape? But the moon isn't even out yet."

"I know, but I like painting on the beach when I can. Just hearing the ocean helps me paint better, I think." Stella tilted her head to the side and studied her painting with a frown. "Painting water is the hardest thing I've ever done. It's all about finding the light and the dark and figuring out how to shape it, and I haven't quite mastered it yet."

"Wow." Liza sat down in the sand and wrapped her arms around her knees. "That's kind of poetic."

"It is, isn't it? I didn't mean it to be, but it sounds like something a therapist would say." Stella laughed. "Art is my therapy, I suppose."

"Cooking is mine. Though, I haven't been doing it as much lately."

"But you're a caterer." Stella raised a brow, confused.

"I do it for work, sure," Liza said. "But I used to cook for myself. I'd try new recipes and bake interesting things. I liked to explore and play. Now, I just do it for the paycheck. I still like it, but it doesn't bring me the same passion."

"I totally understand that. I stopped painting for years. *Many* years." Stella shook her head and sighed. "I got so wrapped up in the 'important' things in life that I forgot what was really important. I forgot to take care of myself. To do things I loved simply because I loved them."

Liza wrapped her arms more tightly around her legs, feeling vulnerable in a way she hadn't in a long time. Even though Stella wasn't talking about her directly, Liza felt like her shell had been cracked open.

"Why did you start painting again?"

"This town," Stella said. "The people in it. And, mostly, because of Georgia." She laughed. "That woman has a way of knowing what's best for you even if you don't know it for yourself. She's a good one."

"I can tell. She invited me to the book club after knowing me for less than five minutes. Not many people would do that."

"She has a gift." Stella dabbed the tip of her brush in some paint and painted the crest of a wave. On the palette, the color looked gray. Liza thought Stella was about to make a mistake adding it to her pristine canvas. But as soon as she swiped it over the waves she'd already painted, the color popped against the dark blues of the ocean. It seemed to shine with the white light of the moon.

"Speaking of which..." Stella lowered her brush and turned to Liza. Her mouth was twisted in a nervous knot to one side. "I saw Georgia today, and she mentioned you had a plumbing issue last night."

Liza quickly relayed what it was like walking down the hallway to the bathroom and stepping in a puddle, and Stella laughed. Then, she turned more serious.

"Georgia also mentioned one of the guests at the inn offered to help you with the problem. A very handsome guest. A guest you seemed to have some sort of...history with?" Stella seemed uncomfortable with her prying all at once and held up her hands, palms out. "It isn't any of my business, of course. She just said she noticed a little something between the two of you, and she has a sixth sense about those types of things."

Liza could hear her heart beating in her ears, but she didn't know why. Stella wasn't asking anything intensely personal. It was a simple question with a simple answer: *We used to date.* Yet, Liza couldn't give it. Just as she hadn't wanted to discuss their history with Dora on the phone or with Ben himself, Liza didn't want to discuss it with anyone. *Not in a house or with a mouse or on a train or in the rain.*

"We knew each other a long time ago, but I'm working to focus on my future. That's why I came to Willow Beach, after all," Liza said. "To forget the past and focus on the future. That's the best thing I can do for myself."

Stella nodded. "I understand that. Like I said, it's not my business, anyway. Georgia just worried she put you in an awkward position."

"Maybe a bit, but it was fine. He kept the house from flooding, so I can't be upset with her."

The two women fell into an easy silence. Stella painted delicate details on her painting that initially seemed redundant and unnecessary, but after a few minutes, the painting had taken on a whole new level of realism. Liza could see why Stella was the artist and she wasn't.

After a few minutes, Stella sighed and turned to Liza. "I never intended to end up in Willow Beach. I didn't even plan to visit here."

"How did you end up here, then?"

"My car broke down and Sam came to tow me to his shop." She smiled at the memory. "I had big plans to go to Boston, actually. I wanted to figure out what my future held and find my passion again, and Willow Beach didn't factor into my plans at all. But now, it's the best thing that has ever happened to me. I'm happier here than I've ever been and not a single one of my plans panned out."

"That's amazing."

"It is," Stella agreed. "I told you your life is none of my business, and I meant that. We hardly know one another, so take all of my advice with a grain of salt. But take it from someone who always likes to be in control: you can't control destiny. No matter your plans, what is meant to be will be, and you're better off not fighting it."

"Ben isn't my destiny." Liza felt immediately guilty for snapping, but she couldn't help it. At one time, she'd thought he was. It had taken her years to get that idea out of her head, and she wasn't going to allow it back in now.

"I didn't meant to imply that he is. I'm sorry if I'm overstepping. It's just...I'm a helper. I like to help people, and I don't always know when to stop."

"I'm sorry for snapping," Liza said. "Sensitive subject, I suppose."

Stella waved a hand, dismissing her apology. "It's fine. I just wanted to convey that sometimes running from our past isn't the answer we think it will be. I needed a fresh start and a new town and new friends. Maybe that's what you need, too...or maybe not. If this town has taught me anything, it's that you have to be open to the lessons life tries to teach you. Otherwise, you'll end up making the same mistakes over and over again."

Liza didn't know if she believed in destiny or even that life had lessons to teach you. In her experience, things happened, and you could learn from them, but there wasn't necessarily a larger purpose. Unlike the romance book the book club was reading, life didn't make narrative sense. Characters disappeared without closure and people who would one day be married met without any flare of sparks or love at first sight. There wasn't always a rhyme or reason to things, and Liza didn't feel comfortable leaving herself to be caught in the current of life when, instead, she could command her own future.

Still, she thanked Stella for her well-intentioned words, and the two of them were discussing the upcoming holiday season in Willow Beach—the decorations and upcoming parades and festivals—when footsteps on the sand made them both turn around.

A man in a button-down shirt, jeans, and a flannel coat over top was walking towards them. A smile spread across his face when his eyes met Stella's. *This must be Sam*, Liza thought.

Their connection was obvious. It took a full thirty seconds before Sam pulled his gaze away from Stella to introduce himself to Liza.

"You're the woman staying in Mrs. Albertson's house, right?" Before Liza could answer, he continued. "She has me driving her car around every couple days, but it would make a lot more sense if you took over the job, as well. Or do you already have a car?"

"He's pleased to make your acquaintance," Stella laughed, nudging Sam in the side.

He smiled sheepishly, his dimples showing. "Sorry. Rude of me. Nice to meet you."

"You, too." Liza smiled. "Actually, I don't have a car, so if you don't think Mrs. Albertson would mind, that would be great."

Sam shook his head. "The way Mrs. Albertson talked about her trip, I don't think she's sparing a single thought for her house or her car back home."

"She's in France, right?" Stella asked. "I'd love to go to France. Painting the countryside there would be a dream."

A gleam lit up Sam's eyes and he wrapped an arm around Stella and pulled her close. "For our honeymoon."

Stella rolled her eyes and grinned. "According to you, our honeymoon is going to be an entire world tour. It would be easier to keep track of where you *don't* want to go."

"I'll take you wherever you want to go," he whispered.

Liza felt uncomfortable being part of such an intimate moment—especially one that had shades of what Ben said to her in those first days and weeks, so many years ago. She stepped away, ready to bid them both farewell.

"It was nice to meet you, Sam, and wonderful to talk to you again, Stella. I will see you—"

"Oh, don't go," Stella said. "Have you eaten yet? Sam is actually here to pick me up and take me to Georgia's for dinner. I know she'd want you to join us just as much as I do."

Liza was about to mention that she'd just eaten lunch, but that wasn't true. Her conversation with Stella had lasted longer than she thought, and the sun was beginning to set. It was time to think about her next meal, and she still wasn't ready to go into town and risk seeing Ben. However, she also didn't want to go to the inn and chance seeing him there, either.

As though reading her thoughts, Stella said, "Georgia doesn't make dinner for the guests. They all have to fend for themselves. We usually eat in the kitchen, where no one bothers us."

With that, Liza couldn't think of a single reason to say no.

She wouldn't take Stella's advice where it concerned Benjamin Boyd, but Liza figured there was no harm in going with the flow in a few areas of her life.

"Sure, why not."

Stella laughed and began packing up her painting supplies. "That's the spirit."

～

Despite Stella's assurance that Liza wouldn't see any of the guests at the inn, Liza still spent the first half hour in Georgia's kitchen turning her head at every noise, certain Ben would reappear at any second. When he didn't, she finally relaxed enough to begin to enjoy herself.

"If there isn't enough for me, I had a big lunch," Liza said. "I ate an entire personal pizza."

"Nonsense. I've been cooking for a family of five for almost thirty years, and I have to feed an entire inn full of guests breakfast every day. My ability to gauge serving sizes is shot." Georgia laughed. "Stella could have invited half the town, and we'd still have enough."

"What are we having, anyway?" Stella asked. "I stopped listening after you mentioned there would be wine."

"I'm not entirely sure, to be honest." Georgia peeked into the pot on the stove and wrinkled her nose. "It's a new recipe, but I think I've already ruined it. Is it possible to overcook rice?"

Liza walked over to the stove and assessed the situation.

"Well, Chef?"

"I'm not a chef," Liza said. "Not anymore, anyway. But I'd be happy to help with whatever you need."

Georgia jumped back immediately as though she was letting go of a hot potato. "I'd like all the help you're willing to give. Take it away."

Again, Liza was worried about overstepping or being an inconvenience, but it became immediately clear that Georgia was happy to hand over the reins in her own kitchen. Within ten minutes, she was sitting on a stool next to Stella, both of them watching Liza cook.

The rice Georgia had started making was a little soggier than Liza usually liked her rice, but it was an easy fix. Liza poured in a few cups of chicken stock, lowered the heat, and put the lid back on. With a bit more steaming, the rice would begin to break down into porridge.

Liza cracked the lid open a few times to throw in slivers of fresh ginger and pinches of various spices and herbs, but mostly, she focused on the chicken.

The chicken breasts were large and different shapes, so Liza butterflied them, laid them between two layers of plastic wrap, and pounded them flat so they'd cook more evenly.

"That has got to be good stress relief," Georgia said, reaching for the mallet and giving the meat a few good whacks herself. She nodded in approval. "Yep. That's satisfying."

"This is why cooking is my therapy." Liza winked at Stella, who laughed.

"Much better than painting. I can't take a hammer to a canvas."

Georgia had already seasoned the outside of the meat with kosher salt, so Liza squeezed some fresh lime juice over the chicken breasts and let them marinate in the juice for a few minutes while she heated up a skillet and softened onions and garlic. Then, she threw in the chicken and let it sizzle in the pan.

Liza got so lost in the process of cooking that she forget she had a rapt audience. She forgot everything.

For a few minutes, cooking felt the way it used to. Part of it, Liza suspected, came from the fact that she had to problem solve. Georgia had ingredients, but no direction, so Liza was left to arrange the ingredients into a meal like a puzzle. Seeing a meal come together like that was one of Liza's favorite things.

Once the chicken was cooked, Liza sliced the breasts into strips and laid them on top of heaping bowls of fragrant rice porridge. Then, she sprinkled on chopped cilantro and slices of jalapeño.

Georgia and Stella both dove in before Liza could even make herself a plate.

"Oh my goodness." Stella clamped a hand over her mouth, and Liza worried for a moment she'd made something inedible.

Georgia, too, gasped and stared at Liza, eyes wide.

"Is it good?" Liza asked. "Is it too spicy? Undercooked? Is it—"

"It's *incredible.*" Georgia shook her head and ate another bite, nodding as if to confirm her first opinion.

"I've made a thousand different meals with chicken and rice, but I've never made anything like this," Stella said.

"It's a basic variation of Khao Tom Gai."

"*She says casually,*" Georgia quipped. "I've never even heard of it before."

"I hadn't either until I catered a luncheon for a Thai community center in Boston. It was in the early days of my business, and I made a very runny risotto. To make me feel better, one of the men told me it reminded him of his mother's Khao Tom Gai. So, I told him to have her send me the recipe."

"And she did?" Stella asked.

"She did one better. She called and talked me through the process step by step on the phone." Liza hadn't thought of that memory in years, and she couldn't help but smile. "It took over an hour, so she told me about immigrating here in her twenties and raising her children when she barely knew the language. It made my problems feel much more manageable. Her name was Apinya, and we kept in touch for years until she passed away."

"That's beautiful," Georgia said softly, looking back down at her bowl as though it held new meaning. She scooped out a spoonful and held it aloft. "To Apinya."

"To Apinya," Liza and Stella echoed.

As the women ate, they talked easily, and Georgia expressed interest in Liza finding the time to host a cooking class at the inn. It seemed Georgia was constantly experimenting with new ways to entertain her guests, and Liza was honored to even be considered. More than that, though, Liza was reminded why she loved food.

Cooking and eating created a shared experience. It made new memories and created the opportunity to share old ones. Food tore down borders and walls and generational gaps. Every person on earth needed to eat, and food and the need for it was the one thing people had in common.

When Liza stopped and thought about it, she couldn't imagine how she could ever lose her passion or motivation for cooking. Food was life, and there were few things more important than that.

10

When Liza's phone went off the next morning and Stacy's name appeared on her screen, Liza's heart jumped.

Since her dinner with Stacy and Ben, Liza hadn't spent any time imagining the menu for her reception or coming up with ideas. As they parted, Stacy had mentioned calling Liza in a few days to discuss things more in depth, but Liza had been distracted with Ben and the pipe bursting.

She considered not answering, but decided that would look much more unprofessional than answering the call and telling the truth. So, Liza picked up just before her phone would usually send the call to voice mail.

"Stacy! Hello. It's so good to hear from you. How are you—"

"Oh, Liza," Stacy interrupted, sounded exasperated. "I'm so glad you answered. I'm in a bit of a bind, and I had no one else to call."

Liza frowned. "Is everything okay?"

In all her years catering weddings and big events, Liza had received more than her fair share of panicked calls from frazzled clients.

Though, usually, they came on the day of the event when they realized they didn't have enough tables or chairs or tablecloths. Or, one time, when the venue caught on fire the night before and the entire party had to be relocated to a moose lodge across town that didn't have an in-house kitchen. In the end, Liza cooked everything in her kitchen office downtown and then had a fleet of cars driven by Angela's college friends deliver the food to the venue, where it was kept warm until dinnertime. It wasn't her best work, but under the circumstances, the client was thrilled.

"Yes, sorry." Stacy laughed. "I'm sure you deal with people all the time who think their minor drama is the end of the world, and I don't want to be one of those people."

"You aren't," Liza said, despite what she'd just been thinking. "Just tell me what you need, and I'll do my best to help."

"I was supposed to drive into Willow Beach today after lunch to meet with the alcohol supplier, but my boss just tasked me with leading a big meeting with out-of-town clients, so I can't make it. I know it is a lot to ask of you, but since you are doing the food, I thought maybe you'd be able to sit in on the meeting for me? You already know all of the details of the event, so could you just pass that information along and make sure the supplier isn't a criminal? Is that too much? It's too much. I'm sorry. I—"

"Stacy, it's not too much. Really. I deal with this kind of stuff all the time. It isn't any trouble."

Stacy let out a long sigh of relief. "Are you sure? I don't want to be a burden. And I'll pay you for the trouble."

"Who's your alcohol supplier?"

Liza could hear papers rustling on the other side of the line as Stacy shuffled through things before finally answering. "Oh, here it is. It's the Duke Saloon. The woman I talked to was named—"

"Alma," Liza finished.

"You know her?"

"As it so happens, I do. I just met her the other day, and I can confirm she isn't a criminal. Not an obvious one, at least."

Another sigh of relief through the phone. "Wow, that's amazing. Thank you so much, Liza. You're a lifesaver."

Liza didn't think this task would save any lives, exactly, but it would save her client's sanity, which seemed important as well. Plus, Liza liked what she'd seen of Alma so far, and she would be glad to get to know her more.

~

Later in the afternoon, Liza pulled a pair of leather booties on over her jeans, a long coat on over her cowl-necked sweater, and a knit hat over her hurriedly brushed hair, and walked into town.

The weather radar didn't show any signs of snow, but Liza could smell frost in the air. Everything smelled crisp and clean, and she blew puffs of air in front of her face as she walked, watching them dissolve into the sky.

It felt strange to be going to a saloon alone before dinner, but after her cold walk, Liza couldn't think of anything nicer than wrapping her hands around a steaming hot toddy.

After her walk in the bright November sun, Liza had to pause in the doorway to let her eyes adjust to the dimness inside. The only lights came from the can lights above the tables and the lights at the bar, but Liza could see the saloon had an obvious southern theme. Barrels were used in place of chairs at several tables, lassos and horseshoes hung from the wood-paneled walls, and speakers were playing country music softly in the background.

"Hello there! Are you here for business or pleasure?" Alma came strolling out of the kitchen in bootcut jeans, red-tipped cowboy boots, and a button-down shirt with pearl buttons. She saw Liza's attention turn to her clothes and gave a small spin. "I know, I know. It's a little much, but occasionally I ham it up for the sake of theme."

"You look great," Liza said. "And I suppose I'm here for a bit of both. You had a meeting with Stacy Boyd this afternoon?"

"Oh, that's right. The bride. Is she coming later?"

"She's stuck at work, so I'm here as a substitute."

Alma grinned and waved Liza towards a booth. "No offense to her, but I'm much more excited to be sitting down with you. Brides are often a bit too high-strung for my taste. They act like I don't know how to run an open bar. Hello? I do it every night."

Liza laughed. "I'm excited, too. We didn't get to talk much at the book club meeting. Plus, I'm frozen, and I'd love a hot drink."

"With alcohol?"

"Please," Liza nodded.

Alma turned over her shoulder and opened her mouth to shout before she stopped and sighed. "Darn. For a second, I almost forgot I'm the only one working the bar right now. I'll be right back."

Liza settled into a booth while Alma dashed behind the bar and made two drinks.

Alma slid two double-walled glass mugs onto the table and slid into the bench seat opposite Liza. Both drinks had a slice of lemon floating on the surface of the water, but Liza's was a noticeably darker color.

"Hot water with lemon and honey," Alma explained. "I operate a bar, but I try to avoid drinking too much. If I had a drink with every person I sat down with during the day, my liver would be toast. Yours has some black rum. It's my favorite spirit for the colder months."

Liza took a sip and sighed. The spiced rum had a nice warmth that was amplified by the honey and then undercut by the lemon. Perfectly balanced in every way.

"There's not much to talk about in terms of the wedding," Alma said, getting straight to the point. "Stacy wanted two open bars on either end of the reception hall. She is going to buy the alcohol and then keep whatever is left over, so I'll send her my recommendation per her number of guests and see what she decides. Myself and another of my bartenders here will run the bars all night, and our price is $30 per hour. Again, I'll write all of this up in the email to Stacy. Do you need anything else?"

Liza squinted, trying to think of anything she could possibly ask Alma. "Um, are you a criminal?"

Alma raised one brow in surprise and then threw her head back and laughed. "No, darling, I most certainly am not."

"I think that's all the information I need, then," Liza shrugged with a smile. "You have all of the details of the wedding already, and she wanted me to make sure you aren't a criminal. Check and check."

"To a job well done." Alma lifted her mug for a toast, and they clinked glasses. "Now, for the fun."

"Fun" for Alma involved a good dose of gossip. As a business owner in the town and a bartender, she knew a tremendous amount of information about people's personal lives.

"You'd be surprised how many people show up here, get a little tipsy, and then give you their entire life story," she said. "And if you want to know who the criminals around here are, the sheriff is a regular, and he has told me everything. This town is nice and shiny on the surface, but underneath, there's a dark underbelly."

Liza frowned. "There is?"

She didn't know Willow Beach incredibly well yet, but she'd pictured it as the kind of cheery, sparkly town you'd see in a made-for-TV movie. Everyone was nice and friendly, and you'd never imagine it could be a place with much criminal activity or violence.

Perhaps, though, she'd been wrong.

"Oh yeah," Alma continued, leaning forward. "Last week, the sheriff got a call that the mill where Katie at Good Stuff Cupcakes gets her sugar isn't certified organic, so her organic lemon bars are anything but. *Very* juicy stuff."

Alma rolled her eyes, and Liza cackled. "For a second, I thought you were serious about the seedy underbelly."

"I wish. It would make my job a lot more interesting." She sipped her lemon water. "I hear about relationship problems all day long, but just the mundane stuff. Mostly money, honestly. Everything around here is dull."

Despite Alma's claims, she had more than enough stories to keep Liza entertained for over an hour. Once, a pastor from the next town over dropped by the bar for the explicit purpose of praying for Alma's soul. In his opinion, anyone who made alcohol their living was in desperate need of salvation.

"He nearly fell off his stool when I told him my brother is the pastor of a Baptist church back home in Texas," she laughed.

Alma also talked about Georgia's past, though that conversation sounded less gossipy and much more like a friend being worried about her friend.

"She is happy with Joel—I can see that—but I'm still worried about her. She and Richard were together for a long time, and I don't think you get over something like that overnight. I keep expecting to get a middle-of-the-night sobbing phone call from her, but it hasn't happened yet. I haven't seen her cry at all."

"It took me almost a year to accept that I was divorced," Liza said.

Alma didn't yet know about Liza's relationship history, so she filled her in briefly.

"Twenty years." Alma whistled when she was done and shook her head. "I'm so sorry."

Liza shrugged. "It's okay, really. Even if I didn't expect it, I wasn't entirely surprised. It made sense when I really thought about it. Neither of us had been happy for a while. Maybe Georgia's situation is like that, too."

Alma looked unsure. "I don't think so. From what everyone could see, she and Richard were a good pair. She said later that he'd been a bit more detached, but she didn't see it coming at all, so it's hard to imagine she's moved on already. Part of me thinks it may be because all of her kids are in relationships now. It has to be hard to have your relationship fall apart at the same time everyone around you is finding love."

The two women each sipped at their drinks. Liza felt the beginnings of a pleasant buzz circulating through her system.

"Don't get me wrong," Alma added. "I'm so happy for her and Joel, and I want them to be happy. They make a good couple."

"You just want what's best for your friend."

"Exactly. I want her to process the pain from her past before she forges ahead. I don't want this coming back to bite her."

As dinnertime approached, Alma needed to get back to the bar and the kitchen. The saloon's evening staff were showing up for their shifts and patrons were coming in after work. Alma thanked Liza for a good conversation, made her promise she'd come in so they could chat again sometime, and then slid out of the booth and walked back to the bar.

Alma walked down to the far end of the bar, where two men had just come in and sat down. Liza followed her with her eyes—and when she saw who'd entered, her heart jumped into her throat.

She recognized Stella's fiancé, Sam, when he turned his head slightly to talk to Alma, but the other man didn't need to turn around for Stella to know who he was. From the back, especially—ignoring the salt and pepper hair—Benjamin Boyd looked exactly the same as he had all those years ago. Same broad shoulders, same tanned neck, same spiraled cowlick on the crown of his head.

Alma said something to Sam and pointed back at the booth where Liza was still sitting, and both men turned around to look in her direction.

Liza jolted, turning her eyes away, even though everyone had seen her looking. Then, realizing how ridiculous she looked, she turned back and smiled, locking her eyes on Sam and avoiding Ben entirely.

Clearly, Liza shouldn't be giving Georgia Baldwin any advice. She had some unresolved issues of her own to deal with.

Sam smiled and waved her over, and Liza didn't see a way she could refuse him without looking rude. She was sitting in a booth alone. She could tell him she had other plans and needed to leave, but regardless, she'd have to go over there to tell him to his face. Unless she wanted to run from the building without explanation, she had no other choice.

Liza walked towards the bar with a weight sitting heavy in her stomach.

"It's nice to see you again, Liza," Sam said. "Alma said you made a fun drinking partner. Would you care to sit with us? Ben here isn't nearly as lively as I hoped he'd be."

"Perhaps I should leave then. I don't think Liza's opinion of me will be any more favorable." Ben said the words cheerily enough and nudged

Sam's shoulder playfully, but there was something in his tone that made everyone, including Liza, look at him.

His beer was only a quarter gone, but he was getting ready to get up and walk out. It would look suspicious if he did, and Liza didn't want to explain anything to anyone. She didn't believe Alma would share her business with anyone, but still, Liza didn't want to be just another piece of gossip Alma had gathered while working the bar.

"Oh, you two know each other?" Sam asked.

Liza nodded. "We're old friends, and he's being silly. I'd be the first to tell anyone who asked that Ben knows how to have fun. How long the fun lasts is up for debate, but—"

She regretted the words immediately, and based on the hush that fell over the group, she knew she'd made them uncomfortable, too.

Thankfully, Ben forged ahead through the tension. "Well, tonight the fun will last at least until after dinner. Order something. It's on me. You too, Sam."

Sam and Liza both tried to refuse, but Ben insisted, and Liza felt guilty leaving after she'd behaved so poorly and Ben had responded so graciously. So, she finally relented and sat down.

A group of two young couples sitting against the back wall got up and turned the jukebox on. They chose an aggressively loud disco song, and Alma wrinkled her nose.

She grumbled about unplugging the jukebox when she dropped off their menus, and Liza had to agree. She'd never been a fan of disco.

Liza decided on the biscuits and gravy before she was even halfway through the first page. Breakfast for dinner had always been one of her favorites. Ben ordered the chicken-fried steak, and Sam was about to place his order when his phone rang.

"Excuse me," he said, stepping away from the bar and taking the call. Less than a minute later, he came back, closed his menu, and slid his wallet into his back pocket. "I'm sorry to dash, but someone accidentally threw the wrong set of car keys into the overnight drop-off box and is now trapped in the parking lot. I have to go rescue them."

"We can wait for you," Ben offered.

"No, no. Go ahead and eat. Rain check." Sam gave them a three-fingered wave and hurried out the door.

Had this been planned? Liza wondered.

No, certainly not. It would be a very elaborate plan if so. And why would Sam participate in it even if Ben had wanted to get Liza alone?

This was probably just as uncomfortable for Ben as it was for Liza. If anything, Liza should cancel her order and leave now, too. It would be the best option for both of them.

"Well, just the two of us." Ben neatly stacked their menus and folded his hands in front of him on the bar top as the disco song began playing for a second time.

Liza studied him for a minute, trying to gauge his emotions. It proved to be a grave mistake.

From the first time she'd met Ben, Liza had never been able to read him. No matter the situation, Ben looked calm. Unlike Liza, he had an amazing poker face. It was part of the reason Liza hadn't seen their breakup coming.

Now, on top of feeling uncomfortable having dinner with Ben for the second time in less than a week, Liza was also dwelling on the past *and* watching his jaw clench and unclench, wondering if it was because of her. She couldn't see any signs of discomfort on his face, but she knew better than anyone that that didn't mean he wasn't uncomfortable. So, what should she do?

I don't want to talk to you again.

That was one of the last things Liza had said to Ben. She'd made her feelings pretty clear. Should she reiterate those feelings and leave, embarrassing Ben in front of Alma? Or should she stay calm and tough it out the way Ben seemed intent on doing?

Suddenly, Ben leaned towards her slightly, talking quietly out of the side of his mouth. "I didn't plan this."

"What?"

"This," he said, gesturing to the two of them and the bar. "Stacy wants a vintage car to take her and Jonathan from the wedding to the reception, and Georgia told me Sam would be my best bet. I met with him this afternoon, and he invited me for a drink. I didn't know you'd be here."

"Stacy asked me to come talk to the alcohol distributer since she got stuck at work," Liza explained. "I didn't know you'd be here, either."

Ben nodded and pressed his lips together. "Good. I just wanted you to know I heard you when you said you don't want to talk to me. Though, I do hope we can endure each other's presence enough to get through one meal. I'm still paying."

Was he angry with her? Again, Liza couldn't tell. It would make sense considering the way she'd treated him. He'd helped her with a plumbing issue in the middle of the night, and Liza had thanked him by *not* thanking him and then telling him to stay away from her. On some level, she felt he deserved it, but on another level, she was a grown adult who should be able to rise above thirty-year-old drama.

"I can pay for my own food."

"I know you can, but I already offered, and I don't want Alma to think I'm a flake."

That was a good reminder. This was about appearances. Neither of them wanted to be here, but there was no need to cause any drama before Stacy's wedding. Liza was the caterer, Ben was the brother of honor, and Liza wouldn't do anything to cause tension on Stacy's special day. She was being paid to make her life easier, not more awkward.

"Did the plumber fix the leak?" Ben asked, moving into the casual conversation portion of the meal.

"He wasn't very happy to have an unscheduled repair first thing in the morning, but he got it taken care of, yes. The place smells a little musty still, but the leak is fixed and there wasn't enough water to cause any serious damage, so I think it's all fine."

"Good. That's great."

Liza chewed on the inside of her cheek and kicked the toes of her shoes against the wood-paneled bar front. Finally, after a long silence, she burst out, "Thank you. For helping that night, I mean. I'm sorry if I was harsh."

Ben turned towards her, mouth pulled up in a smirk. "How much did that hurt?"

"What?"

"Apologizing."

Liza narrowed her eyes at him, regretting her momentary weakness.

He chuckled. "I didn't think I'd ever hear those words from you."

"Yeah, well, don't get used to them."

For the third straight time, the disco song started playing again, and Alma slammed her hand on the far end of the bar and shouted at the young couples responsible, "Enough with the disco!"

The boys laughed, but their girlfriends looked embarrassed.

Alma slid a quarter to Ben. "Please play something else. I can't take this song again."

His elbow brushed against Liza's arm as he got up, and Liza felt a warmth emanating from him. He moved with grace and ease, the same way he handled everything in his life. When Liza was frozen with indecision, worried about what to say or do, Ben always had a comeback or a retort. He wasn't awkward or uncertain of himself.

That was probably a side effect of being the dumper rather than the dumpee, Liza figured. He had the upper hand, so why should he be awkward? Liza was the one who had to prove her life hadn't been miserable without him. She was the one who had to prove she was fine and didn't need him.

Ben didn't need to prove anything.

He walked over to the jukebox and leaned against it, one of his hands drumming the side as he selected a song.

Liza recognized the piano intro immediately, and she spun towards Ben just as he turned away from the jukebox. If there was any chance he'd chosen the song by random, it dissolved as soon as Liza saw his face.

He remembered what the song meant to them, and he'd selected it on purpose.

"Chicago?" Alma gave him a thumbs-up. "Amazing choice."

Ben sat down next to Liza, avoiding her eyes for the first time. "Thanks. 'You're the Inspiration' is one of my all-time favorites."

As the first verse gave way to the chorus, déjà vu washed over Liza. Alma was tapping her fingers and Ben was bobbing his head to the beat.

But Liza was busy wishing she could be literally anywhere else.

11

Thirty Years Earlier

"You don't have to stick around," Liza said as she passed the table where Ben had been sitting all night. "As soon as this group finishes dinner, I'm going to close and leave."

"I'll wait."

"I'm going to go straight home and go to sleep. I open at the photo lab first thing."

Ben nodded. "I'll wait."

She sighed like she was exasperated, but Ben's attention thrilled her. He doted on her, and everyone noticed. The other waitresses complained that their boyfriends never stuck around until closing just to walk them to their car. Liza reminded them Ben wasn't her boyfriend, but then...what was he?

He came into the restaurant and spent an ungodly amount of money on food and drinks he didn't want just so her manager would let him keep his table in her section. He slipped Liza notes whenever she passed, telling her how pretty she looked, asking for the next day she had off so they could make plans, and occasionally requesting she change the channel of the television over the bar so he could watch the game he wanted to watch.

It had been almost a month of this, yet Ben hadn't made a serious move. He hadn't asked Liza to be his girlfriend or even tried to kiss her. Liza felt certain he liked her, but there was enough room for doubt that she was becoming uncomfortable.

When the last table left, the back-of-the-house staff had already cleared the kitchen for the night, so they left. Liza and Ben were alone in the restaurant.

He wiped down chairs and put them on top of the tables while Liza wiped down glasses behind the bar.

"They must really trust you to let you close up on your own."

"Or really hate me," Liza laughed. "No one likes to close. It's boring and kind of creepy. The quiet is unnerving after so many hours of noise."

"We can fix that." Ben flipped a chair onto a table and then jogged towards the rarely used jukebox in the corner, digging in his pocket for a quarter as he went.

"I don't think that thing even works. No one ever uses it." The previous owners had more of a diner vibe going with the place, but the current owners had turned it into a bar and grill and the place now attracted clientele that were much more interested in hearing the score of the game than music.

Ben dropped his quarter in and the machine lit up, the records inside shuffling. He looked over his shoulder at Liza, eyebrows wagging, and beamed.

He was beautiful. Handsome and manly, but beautiful, too. Liza had been attracted to him from the first time she'd really taken the time to look at him, but that attraction had grown into something more, something deeper. Like a clear mountain stream that had begun as a trickle of water, slowly eating away at the stone, washing it away until you couldn't imagine the mountain without a stream.

Liza couldn't imagine her life without Ben.

When had that happened?

Before Liza could panic about the knot of feelings in her chest, slow piano music started. Ben spun around as the classic eighties chords played, an air guitar in his hands, and Liza laughed.

"No, stop," she said, laughing in anticipation of whatever he was about to do. He had a dangerously mischievous look in his eyes, and if there was one thing Liza knew about Ben, it was that there was no way to know what he had planned.

The music softened, and Ben began lip syncing along with the song, interpretive dancing his way towards her with overwrought facial expressions as the song crooned on about true love and life's meaning and inspiration.

Ben circled around Liza, dragging his hand across her shoulders like they were in a movie musical. Liza couldn't stop herself from laughing, but she also had an army of butterflies setting up camp in her stomach.

"*Now I know that I need you here with me. From tonight until the end of time.*" His singing voice was off-pitch and shaky, but he performed with ridiculous passion, and Liza didn't resist when he finally pulled her into his arms.

Ben spun Liza around the empty restaurant, dancing with the same grace and style he walked through life with. As the song began to fade, the singer's voice growing softer as he repeated, again and again, what it meant to love somebody, Liza wondered if love was what she felt for Ben.

Outside of the restaurant, they'd gone on a drive together and met up with Dora and her boyfriend for a movie, but what else did Liza really know about him?

Immediately, a thousand things sprang into her mind.

Ben was kind and laid-back. He didn't take life too seriously, but in the conversations they'd had while closing, Liza knew Ben had plans. He had dreams of traveling the world and serving humanity in some way. He was confident without being mean. Ben didn't need to put anyone down to feel good about himself, and he was the funniest person she knew without ever making fun of anybody.

Except her, of course. He teased her endlessly, and Liza teased him right back. He brought out a spunky side of her she'd never seen before, and she liked it. Liza liked that life felt more special with Ben in it. He had a way of seeing the world that inspired her to be more forgiving and more patient. He made her want to be a better person.

The music faded back to silence, and Ben's chest rose and fell against hers, his face flushed from dancing.

She looked into his eyes, getting lost in the green of them, and they stood there, frozen for one second and then two. Liza thought he would kiss her, but the moment came and passed, and they pulled away. They both laughed, but there was a tinge of disappointment in the air, too.

Liza went around the restaurant, locking doors and turning off light switches, and when she came back to the dining room, Ben was waiting by the door with her coat. He held it out for her, and she slipped her arms in the sleeves, aware of the way his fingertips brushed across her shoulders.

As soon as she stepped outside, Liza stopped. Ben bumped into the back of her and then gasped, seeing it, too.

"It's snowing," he said. "A lot."

"I had no idea," she whispered.

It felt necessary to whisper. It was late, the road in front of the bar and grill was quiet, and everything was covered in at least six inches of snow.

The flakes were full and heavy, and Liza could hear them hitting the ground, visibly accumulating even in the few seconds they were standing in the doorway.

"It's magical," Liza said, stepping out carefully in her sneakers. She didn't have the right shoes on at all, but the snow was perfect and untouched, and she couldn't resist being the first person to make tracks. "I love the snow."

"Well, that settles it."

"What?" Liza turned to Ben, but he was walking after her, his brows lowered and set, his lower lip tucked between his teeth.

Instead of answering, he grabbed her shoulders, pulled her against him, and lowered his lips to hers.

Liza was too stunned to move for a moment, but she quickly got over it. She wrapped her arms around his neck and sagged against him.

Ben tasted as good as he smelled—like mint and citrus—and his lips were soft, but firm. He kissed with confidence, no sense of hesitation or doubt, and Liza felt like they'd done this a thousand times before. It felt easy and natural, and she missed him the moment he pulled away, smiling down at her.

"Whoa."

Ben laughed and kissed her forehead. "I'm glad you agree. It was whoa for me, too."

Liza felt flustered and flushed. "What was that for?"

"Because I wanted to," he said. "Because I should have done it inside. Because the world feels like a snow globe, and I wanted you to always remember the first time we kissed."

"Snow globe or not, I don't think I could ever forget that."

He laughed again and then grew serious. For the first time, Ben looked nervous. His eyes darted around, and his fingers drummed on her upper arms.

"What is it?" Liza asked.

"Well, there was something else I was going to do, but I seem to have turned into a horrible coward all of the sudden."

"What were you going to do?" The kiss had been more than enough for Liza, so she couldn't imagine anything more than that. Her knees were still trembling from the force of it. Still, she had to know. "Tell me."

Ben's green eyes landed on her and everything seemed to stop. Snowflakes froze in the air, time stilled, and the planet stopped turning on its axis. Liza had never felt more looked at in her entire life. Ben saw her. When he looked at her, he seemed to pierce to her very soul, expose her.

She took a deep breath, trying to prepare for whatever was coming next. It wasn't enough.

"Liza, I'm falling for you. You don't have to say anything, but I just want you to know."

He said it somberly, like he wasn't sure if he should or not, and Liza wanted to laugh.

How could he not know? How could he be self-conscious about this of all things?

Liza wasn't falling for him.

She'd already fallen.

12

Ben sat down while Alma sang along with the song quietly as she worked behind the bar, oblivious to the torment Liza was going through.

For years, she'd turned off movies that used this song in their soundtracks, changed the radio station every time it came on, and done her best to avoid going back to that night with Ben.

It was the night she realized she loved him. It was the night she began making plans, envisioning a future with him, reshaping her hopes and dreams to include him.

It was also—though she didn't know it then—the night Liza took one irreversible step down the path to heartbreak.

This song didn't just represent her good times with Ben; it represented the bad ones, too. It represented the nights she'd spent crying in her room, muffling herself with a pillow so Dora wouldn't hear.

Liza had spent the last thirty years writing Ben out of her life and her memory, and now here he was, crashing back into her consciousness with no warning, and Liza didn't know how to handle it.

"You said you didn't want to talk," he said softly. "So, I'm not talking."

"You decided to torment me via song. Yay me." Liza tried to sound casual, but the words came out strained.

"I'm not trying to torment you, Liza. I'm trying to tell you..."

I love you, whispered a voice in her head.

In real life, Ben said, "I'm sorry." He paused and looked at her curiously. "I'm trying to tell you that I regret what happened with us."

Of course, he didn't love her anymore. He didn't *know* her anymore. Not this version of her, anyway. Why had Liza thought, for even a minute, that was what he was going to say? Absurd. Ridiculous. Impossible.

Still, why did she feel disappointed?

Because you want to crush him the way he crushed you, she thought, surprised by her subconscious desire for vengeance.

That was part of it, sure. It would feel nice if Ben loved her. If Liza could look at him after all these years and tell him to kick rocks. To tell him that he'd missed his chance long, long ago.

Another part of it was loneliness and a desire to have a plan. If any man had shown Liza interest at the bar, she felt confident she'd react the same way. As much as she tried to pretend, for Angela and Dora and everyone else, that she wasn't upset about her divorce from Cliff, Liza was lonely. She wanted someone to lean on and depend on. Someone to wake up next to and talk to about her day.

She wasn't disappointed because it was Ben and she loved him, but because he was a person, and she'd been short a person in her life for the last three years.

"It's been thirty years."

"So?" Ben shrugged. "That doesn't mean I can't still apologize. It doesn't mean I shouldn't apologize. I never told you how sorry I was for how things ended, so I'm telling you now. What we had was special to me, and I shouldn't have thrown it away the way I did."

Liza's throat tightened, and she felt ridiculous. She turned away from him, feigning interest in a couple of men in greasy work shirts coming through the double doors of the saloon. "It's fine."

Ben chuckled softly, and Liza turned around. What could possibly be funny about this situation?

He shook his head like he could read her thoughts. "It's just funny that, after all these years, I can still tell when you're lying."

The song ended, and Liza felt a weight lift off her shoulders. She shifted in her seat and almost clapped when their dinner plates came through the swinging doors of the kitchen, grateful for any distraction.

"I'm not exactly hard to read."

The waiter slid their plates toward them, warning they were hot, and Liza smiled at him. The sooner she ate this food, the sooner she'd get to leave.

As she dug in, Ben mumbled under his breath, "You'd be surprised."

She didn't know what that meant, but she didn't care to ask. They ate mostly in silence, and Liza could only make it halfway through her biscuits and gravy before she had to ask Alma for a doggie bag.

"These are incredible, but if I eat another bite, I'll have to roll myself home."

"You flatter me, Ms. Professional Chef." Alma grabbed her plate and disappeared into the kitchen.

Ben slid his empty plate to the edge of the bar and leaned back. "I can't wait to eat your cooking again at the wedding. You've always been a fabulous cook. You make the best pancakes I've ever had."

"I don't think Stacy would approve pancakes on her wedding menu."

"She would if she tasted them." Ben patted his stomach. "I tried for a while to find a recipe that tasted anything like yours, but I never had any luck. I don't know what your secret ingredient is, but it's a doozy."

Usually Liza would quip, *It's love*, but that hardly felt appropriate. Instead, she thanked him and waited patiently for Alma to bring them the check.

"Was this as horrible as you thought it would be?" Ben asked after a brief pause.

"I didn't think it would be horrible."

"Liar," he laughed. "I saw your face when you spotted me. I thought you were going to make a break for it."

Liza had considered it, but he didn't need to know that.

"I didn't relish the thought of sitting down with you," she admitted, "but it was fine. I don't think you're a bad person, Ben. When I said I didn't want to talk to you the other night, it wasn't because you're horrible or bad company. It's exactly the opposite."

"It's because I'm wonderful and good company?" he asked, chin dimpled in confusion.

Liza shouldn't have said anything, but it was too late to take it back now. She sighed and ran a hand through her hair. Being so close to the ocean had made her curly hair even more unruly than usual. Though, she didn't hate the idea of having beachy waves. It was better than the staticky mess her hair became this time of year in Boston.

"It's the same reason I avoid cheesecake and kettle-cooked chips and big bags of chocolate," Liza said. "It's delicious, but it's not good for me. And in the end, I always end up feeling miserable."

Ben's usually unreadable expression faltered and Liza caught a look of sad regret moving across his brow. In an instant, it was gone.

"Then we'll have to learn moderation." Ben pulled out his phone and slid it towards her. "Type in your number."

Liza looked at the phone like it was actively on fire. "No."

"For wedding purposes," he explained. When it was clear Liza wasn't convinced, he continued. "Okay, or you can text and find out where in town I'm eating so you can avoid me like the plague on humanity I am. How does that sound?"

"Wonderful, if a little dramatic."

Despite the insult, Ben laughed. "But seriously, it might be nice to have your number for the wedding. Stacy is playing it cool now, but she's going to be a disaster on the day. If you have any issues or questions, I'd rather you call me than her. As the bro of honor, it's my solemn duty."

He was making fun, but he wasn't wrong. Liza had been in contact with members of the wedding party regularly in the past, and talking to a bro of honor was preferable to bringing any issue to the bride on her big day.

Liza pursed her lips for a moment and grabbed his phone before she could change her mind. She told herself she'd delete his number as soon as the wedding was over.

Ben smirked, and when he reached for his phone, Liza pulled it back. "This isn't a victory for you. This is about my job, okay?"

"I know," he said, holding up his hands in an unconvincing surrender. "You're very professional, Liza."

Ben had mentioned moderation, and she had clearly overdone it with him tonight. She was ready to leave.

She rolled her eyes and slid his phone to him. "That's Ms. Professional Chef to you."

Without another word, she spun off her stool and left him to pay the bill.

13

As it turned out, Liza didn't need to agonize over giving her phone number to Ben, after all. The next day, while trying to set up a time for a tasting of the wedding menu, Stacy asked Liza to set everything up with her brother instead.

"I'll be there, for sure," Stacy said. "Jonathan is still out of town, but I'll be there. It's just that my schedule is jam-packed all of today, but I'm free as a bird tomorrow. So, text Ben, find out what time works for him, and then I'll be there. Okay? Thanks so much."

Liza didn't have time to argue or come up with an excuse before Stacy hung up, so she was left with a decision: should she call him or send a text?

Calling would be more uncomfortable. Liza didn't know anyone who enjoyed making phone calls. According to Angela, Liza was behind the times in terms of technology, but even at her age, receiving a phone call without warning was stressful.

Texting, however, had its own challenges. Namely, it opened a door Liza thought should remain closed.

If she texted Ben about a wedding thing, he could text her back, and then she'd have to respond. Before she knew it, the whole thing could spiral into casual texting about non-wedding issues, and where would that lead?

In the end, Liza realized it would be easier to reject words typed on a screen than the sound of Ben's voice, so she texted.

Stacy told me to arrange a time for the tasting menu with you. It will be at my house tomorrow. What time works for you?

The three dots showing he was typing appeared immediately, and Liza hated how her heart jumped.

If you want to ask me on a date, you don't have to use my sister as a cover.

She typed a quick response: *Not a date! It's work. Your sister will be there, too.*

He sent a frowning emoji and then, a few minutes later:

Is seven okay?

Liza sighed. *Perfect.*

As soon as the time was arranged, Liza turned her phone on silent and dropped it on the couch. She didn't unmute it until the next morning, and even then, she left it on her bedside table all day. Something about it felt dangerous now. Ben's number in her contacts was like a flashing red self-destruct button, waiting to be pressed.

If Liza had anything to say about it, that button would be waiting for a long time.

∼

Liza didn't like to be overbearing during taste-testing sessions. She preferred to spend her time in the kitchen, readying the next course and letting the clients discuss the food privately, but the cottage didn't exactly allow for privacy. Plus, Stacy wanted Liza there every step of the way.

"You can't spend all day cooking this incredible food and not eat it while it's fresh," she said, patting the seat next to her. "Please. Eat with us."

"Yes, Liza, eat with us," Ben echoed. He smiled, and Liza imagined his teeth gleaming like a predator before a meal.

"These hors d'oeuvres are incredible. What am I eating?"

"Mini beef Wellingtons, bacon-wrapped scallops, and giant mushrooms stuffed with artichoke," Liza said, pointing out each dish. "These will be something substantive for your guests to snack on before the main meal starts. I don't want to leave anyone hungry. You didn't mention any specific diet constraints, but I wanted there to be something for everyone: seafood, red meat, and vegetarian."

"What about those guests who might want pancakes?" Ben asked. His expression was stone serious, but his green eyes glimmered.

Liza barely resisted a glare.

"Ben," Stacy said, elbowing her brother in the arm and rolling her eyes. "I'm not serving pancakes at my wedding."

"That's because you've never had Liza's pancakes."

Liza felt her face flush, and she noticed Stacy's quick look from her brother to Liza. She knew. Ben must have told her about their history. It was possible Stacy had known from the beginning, but Liza couldn't imagine Stacy would knowingly hire her brother's ex-girlfriend to be her caterer.

When Liza and Ben were together, Stacy was living back at home with her parents. Liza never met her nor anyone else in Ben's family. Now, she'd see that as a red flag, but back then, she hadn't thought a thing of it.

"Next course," Liza said, dabbing her mouth with a napkin and heading into the kitchen. "For an appetizer, I thought we could do an Italian wedding soup. It's not too fancy and is easy to serve en masse, but it's also delicious."

"Soup is perfect for a November wedding," Stacy said. "Jonathan's family is Italian, so he'll love that."

"And wedding soup is perfect for a wedding," Ben quipped.

Liza poured out three small bowls and carried them on a plastic tray to the table. "They call it that because of the marriage of all of the ingredients, I think."

"I actually had some when I was in Italy, and I think it was called *minestra maritata*. I could be wrong. It has been so long."

Liza's chest tightened at the mention of Ben's travels.

He'd talked about it when they were dating, his desire to get out and see the world, but Liza had naively assumed they'd see it together. She assumed he'd take her along.

How many places had he gone? How many different countries and customs and ways of life had he experienced?

Liza didn't want to know. The thought stole her appetite.

"Where did you learn about the dish, Liza?" Ben asked.

The true answer was on her honeymoon, actually.

Liza and Cliff didn't have much money, but they drove to Chicago and stayed in Cliff's cousin's tiny apartment in Oak Park. They rode the train into the city every morning and wandered around the city. They were there before The Bean was installed or Millennium Park even existed, but they walked along the river, visited every museum they passed, and ate more deep dish pizza than any one human should consume. After three days of nothing but cheese, Liza convinced Cliff to skip the pizzeria and go to a fancy Italian restaurant. The kind of restaurant he wished he could have proposed in.

They did, and Liza ate some Italian wedding soup and the best ravioli she'd ever had in her life. Cliff ordered another deep dish pizza.

"I had it when I was in Chicago years ago," Liza said out loud, breezing past the question and charging ahead. "I figured we would do this soup with a crunchy bread on the side, and then the main course could be a cheese tortellini with a basil pesto. After the meat in the hors d'oeuvres and the meatballs in the soup, I figured everyone would be ready for some carbs."

"I'm always ready for carbs," Stacy laughed. "And no one does carbs like the Italians."

Liza went back into the kitchen to bring out the tortellini, which had been keeping warm on a low setting in the oven.

"I don't know, sis. I had *pão de queijo* in Brazil that you'd really like. It's a small cheese bread that they eat for breakfast. It's amazing. And, oh," Ben paused to sigh longingly. "Sweet bread in Mexico. And naan! There are so many flavor combinations of naan to be had. I made it my mission to try them all while I was in India, but I don't think it's possible. Gosh, I really do love carbs."

"Okay, show off. Not all of us have traveled around the world. I swear, you could have a show on Food Network." Stacy clapped her hands like she'd just had an amazing idea. "You both should have a show! Ben could annoy everyone with his knowledge of food from around the world, and Liza could cook it—inarguably the most important and impressive of the two. Plus, you two have television-worthy levels of snark. People would tune in."

"I'm not built for television," Liza said quietly, setting plates of tortellini in front of everyone.

Ben tipped his head to the side, assessing her. "It's not like you have a face for radio. I think you'd be great with your own cooking show. For better or worse, people always pay more attention to beautiful people."

Liza froze, eyes locked on her plate, vision fuzzy.

He said it so casually, so easily. Like it meant nothing. Like him calling her beautiful after all these years was normal.

Was it normal?

Liza didn't think so, but perhaps Ben acted this way with all women. Liza knew men like that, who gave compliments easily, who had no problem flirting with any woman who came along.

Likely, for Ben, it didn't mean anything. So, Liza determined in that moment that it wouldn't mean anything to her, either.

Stacy swirled a tortellini around in the pesto with increased concentration. When she popped it in her mouth, she moaned and gave Liza a thumbs-up. "This is incredible."

"But is it what you want for your wedding?" Liza asked. "I want to make sure it's what you envisioned serving your guests on your big day. If you'd rather have something more luxurious or even more casual, please tell me. I'm flexible, and I can do whatever you want."

"No, this is great. I left that decision up to you because I trusted your expertise, and I still do. Everything is perfect, don't you think, Ben?"

Ben chewed slowly on his food and looked up at Liza. His stubble had grown in a bit since Liza had first seen him and patches of gray and white hairs were more obvious around his chin. It wasn't fair that he looked better now than he had when they were young. Somehow, Ben had only grown more attractive with time, his face seeming more balanced and refined. He seemed more solid.

Liza didn't want to know what he thought of her after all this time. He'd called her beautiful, but she'd already decided that meant nothing, so who knew what he was thinking?

Not Liza.

He smiled, his dimples making a pronounced appearance, and nodded. "I agree. Perfect."

～

Liza stood in the doorway, too nervous to step into the kitchen and too proud to back away. She wasn't afraid of Benjamin Boyd.

Yet...

"I said I'd *help* you clean up," Ben said over his shoulder, his arms deep in a sink of dirty dishes. "It would have been rude to leave you to do this on your own, but you also can't leave me to do it on my own. It isn't even my wedding."

"Exactly," Liza said, finally moving into the kitchen. "So you can leave. No need to be here."

"Stacy would have stayed to help, but she has to make the drive back to Boston tonight. She'd never forgive her brother for leaving the caterer in a bind."

"Dishes aren't a bind in my profession," Liza said. "They're a necessary evil."

Ben wiped an arm across his forehead, leaving a small cluster of bubbles behind. "Then I'll exorcise some of the evil so long as you come help me dry."

Standing next to Ben was a bad idea. Sitting across from him for their third meal together had been difficult enough. Even with Stacy there, Liza kept catching herself watching him. It wasn't that he was so handsome she couldn't resist—though, that played a small part. More than anything, Liza was in awe that he was standing in her kitchen. Not even in her kitchen, actually. In the kitchen of a stranger Liza was house-sitting for.

Liza's mom had always said, "God laughs while you're busy making plans," but never had that felt truer than now.

Even with her divorce from Cliff, there had been some sense of inevitability. But seeing Ben in Willow Beach? Eating dinner with him? Washing dishes with him?

Liza had never imagined anything like that could happen. Well, not since she was twenty-four, at least.

And that was the problem.

At one point, Liza had imagined some measure of domestic bliss with Ben, and now, here he was, more handsome than ever and washing her dishes. It put Liza in very dangerous territory on her quest to focus on the future and forget the past.

"Here you go," Ben said, holding up a dripping wet baking sheet.

Liza sighed and grabbed the towel from the rack on the front of the oven. It would be faster and simpler to play along and then kick Ben out once the dishes were done. So, that's what Liza would do.

At least, that's what she planned to do. Until Ben suddenly broke the silence. "I never told my sister about the two of us."

Liza nearly dropped the baking sheet. "What?"

"You and me," he said, scrubbing at the bits of pastry left behind from the beef Wellington. "I never told Stacy that we used to date. She was young at the time, so she didn't care about my personal life, and it just never made sense to bring it up. She had no idea who you were when she hired you."

"I assumed as much. Does she know now?"

"I told her the important parts."

Liza snorted. "I'm dying to know what you think the important parts are."

"I told her we dated in our mid-twenties." He handed her a plate, and their fingers brushed during the transfer. Liza yanked the plate away, nearly dropping it.

"That's it?" Liza could think of several other important details to mention.

Ben sighed and dropped a cup into the soapy water, turning his full attention to Liza. "What else would you have added that I left out? I'm sure you'd love nothing more than to tell me how and why I'm wrong."

Liza had dated a coworker she had at the photo lab. She'd dated a friend of Dora's who played football at the junior college. Liza had dated several noteworthy men in her life.

But the only one she'd loved was Ben. She'd loved him deeply.

He wasn't another ex-boyfriend to her. He was *the* ex-boyfriend. The one who shattered her heart and made her a cynic.

Though, perhaps Ben was on to something. Although all of those things were true, Liza had no desire to say them to Stacy or anyone else. No one needed to know. Regardless of what had happened between them, Liza was fine.

Yes, her marriage had ended in divorce after twenty years.

Yes, she'd never had children like she'd always imagined.

Yes, she'd given up her lease and was technically homeless outside of the cottage on the beach she was house-sitting.

Liza's life was a mess, but in every other way...she was fine. And that was all Ben needed to know.

She shrugged. "I would have mentioned something about how you let the most amazing person you ever knew go and how you've regretted it every day since and how time has only made her more luminous."

Liza was teasing Ben and deflecting the seriousness of her feelings all at the same time, but when she looked up at Ben, he was staring at her, his green eyes wide and blinking. He looked like he'd been hit upside the head with a frying pan, dazed and distant.

"I was kidding," Liza said quickly. "I don't think you actually feel that way. It was a joke. Just a joke."

He actually shook his head slightly, blinked, and then shaped his face into a smug mask. "Did I forget to mention it? I did tell Stacy all of those things. Every single word. You nailed it."

"Ha ha." Liza rolled her eyes and took the last cup from Ben, drying it off as he pulled the plug on the sink.

They were done. He could leave.

He wiped his hands on the towel and, rather than heading for the door, leaned back against the counter and crossed his arms over his chest. He had on a flannel button-down with gray pants, and he looked like a hip lumberjack. All he needed was suspenders and a stocking cap.

"There's nothing left to clean," Liza said, gesturing around the kitchen. "You can go now."

He sucked in his cheeks for a second and then, as if deciding something all at once, he pushed off from the counter and crossed the room to stand in front of Liza. She stepped away from him on instinct.

"Go out with me."

She screwed up her face. "Now?"

"No. Tomorrow."

She stared at him, hoping for more clarity, but his grassy-green eyes revealed nothing. "Why? Is it for the wedding or—"

"It's for me," he said. "For us. I think we should go out...together."

Liza shook her head, hardly believing what she was hearing. "Just a few days ago, I told you I didn't want to talk to you anymore. Why would I go out on a date with you?"

"Because fate has brought us together again, Liza, and I don't want to ignore it."

Hearing the word "fate" fall from Ben's lips hit Liza like a knife in the chest. It hurt. It tore down her walls and reminded her of the naïve girl she'd once been.

"Your sister's wedding brought us here."

"No, this cottage on the beach brought you here," Ben pointed out. "Stacy's wedding is just a way to occupy your time. Imagine if Stacy and Jonathan had decided to get married in another small town? Or if Jonathan had been able to push back his business trip? If he had, I wouldn't be here. Stacy wouldn't have needed my help, and I'd still be at home."

"Coincidences aren't fate." Liza crossed her arms and took another step back. "And even if it was fate, crossing paths doesn't mean we need to do anything more than say hello and keep on moving."

He twisted his mouth to the side and narrowed his eyes. "Fine. Then go on a date with me and prove it."

"Prove what?" she asked. "People have been talking about fate and destiny for centuries. I don't think I'll be able to disprove it over dinner."

"Prove that there's nothing between us anymore," he said. "Let's go to dinner, without any other people or leaking pipes or wedding tasks, and talk. Just talk with me for a few hours as friends, and I'll leave you alone."

Friends. Liza had called Ben that once.

When Dora saw him sitting in her section for the third night in a row, she'd teased Liza about her new boyfriend. *He's just a friend*, Liza had said. It was true at the time, though it didn't stay true for long.

Would the same thing happen again?

Not in one night, Liza thought. Ben was charming, but in one night, even he couldn't undo all of the damage he had done.

"You'll leave me alone?" Liza asked.

"If that's what you want."

"Oh, it's what I want." She spun on her heel and marched to the front door, pulling it open and gesturing for him to go.

He listened, walking all the way to the door and stopping in the threshold. "So?"

"So, don't be late. Pick me up at six and have me home by nine."

Ben grinned, and a dormant part of Liza's heart fluttered. He stepped onto the porch and then turned to her and doubled over in a deep bow. "Good night, my lady."

Liza shut the door before he could stand all the way back up.

14

Liza thought the worst part of the evening would be Ben picking her up for the date and dropping her off. That was when they'd be alone. It would be the part of the evening where she'd be forced to sit in the enclosed space of his car, wrapped in the scent of him, and only inches away from the electricity that seemed to pulse from his very center.

As it turned out, Liza had underestimated Ben.

He picked her up at six sharp, wearing dark blue pants, a light gray button-down, and a burgundy bomber jacket. His facial hair had been groomed down to a thin stubble, and his hair was parted on the side, patches of gray and white hairs visible along his temples.

He looked good. Liza had to remind herself that it didn't matter.

This wasn't a normal date. She and Ben weren't going out to test the waters and see if they liked one another. It was more like they were going out to tour the shipwreck of what once had been.

Liza knew she could like Ben. She'd liked him all those years ago, and it seemed many of the qualities she admired then still remained. The difference was, Liza knew what it felt like to lose Ben, and she had no desire to go back there again.

No, this date was simply a way to prove to Ben that Liza had fully moved on. Thirty years separated them from their breakup, and Liza was not in Willow Beach to regress.

She would be moving forward. Without Ben.

"Gorgeous," Ben said, staggering back from the porch steps dramatically, a hand on his heart. "You're a picture, Liza, dear."

Liza had pulled out her forest-green sweater dress for the occasion. It was form-fitting and flattering while also still being stretchy and breathable. Plus, it fell to just below her calves, which meant she could wear flannel leggings rolled up underneath the dress for added warmth.

"Unfortunately," Ben continued, earning a warning eyebrow raise from Liza, "your shoes are not going to work for what I have planned."

"They're booties," Liza said, angling her foot. "Just a tiny heel."

"No heels. Trust me." Ben winked, and Liza's instincts told her to do exactly the opposite. But, despite her doubts, she went inside and put on a pair of white slip-on sneakers.

"Better?"

He grinned and offered his well-toned arm. "Perfect. Shall we?"

Ignoring his arm, Liza walked down the steps and past him to the car. "If we must."

Ben drove the same path Liza usually walked into town. He followed the road along the beach for a while, and Liza expected him to turn onto Eleventh Street to get to Main. When he didn't, she expected he'd take Seventeenth. Yet again, he passed it.

Liza turned to him and frowned. "Where are we going?"

"To dinner."

She hitched a thumb over her shoulder. "The restaurants are all that way. Everything in town is on Main Street."

"Everything *in* town is *in* town, but we aren't going to town." Ben smiled, and Liza's stomach flipped with nerves. What did he have planned?

They drove along the ocean for a while until, finally, Ben turned onto a small dirt road that snaked up the side of a hill. It was barely wide enough for two cars, and trees seemed to press in on other side, blotting out the dying evening light of the sky. Liza tried to remain calm and not ask too many questions—she didn't want to seem nervous—but she didn't like where things were headed.

"There's nothing up here," she repeated. "Where are we going?"

"I'm not taking you to the woods to murder you, if that's what you're worried about."

"I wasn't, but I am now," she mumbled.

Ben chuckled but kept driving.

Finally, the ground leveled out, and Ben turned down an even narrower dirt road and followed it to a small parking lot. Liza was relieved to see another car parked not too far away. At least she knew there'd be someone to hear her scream.

Ben turned the car off and climbed out, but Liza didn't move. When he came around to the passenger side and opened her door, she kept her arms crossed.

"You agreed to this date," he said. "I have three hours before you have to be home. Two hours and fifty minutes, now that we've driven here. You're cutting into my time."

"I'm not getting out until you tell me why I'm about to traipse into the woods. I thought we were going to dinner."

Ben held out a hand to her that Liza refused to take. "We are. Trust me."

Liza snapped her attention to him, jaw set. "Why should I?"

"Because you'll have more fun if you do."

His answer was simple and immediate, but compelling.

Fun.

Liza had almost forgotten what that felt like.

Once again, she ignored his hand and climbed out of the car, smoothing out her dress as she stood. "Fine, but if you're going to make me hunt my own food or gather nuts and berries, I'm stealing your car and leaving you here."

Ben handed her the keys. "I'd expect nothing less."

They walked down a smooth dirt path between trees. The wind was colder up on the hill than down by the beach, and Liza pulled her coat more tightly around her.

"Don't worry. It will be warm where we're going," Ben said.

Liza didn't understand what he meant. From what she could tell, there weren't any buildings around, and last time she'd checked, nature didn't come with a thermostat. She was tired of asking questions she wouldn't get answers to, however, so she stayed quiet and kept moving.

Eventually, the press of trees began to lift so Liza could see a break up ahead. When they reached it, she realized they were standing just above a sheer drop. Below was the road they'd driven up and, beyond that, the ocean. The sky had changed to a washed-out navy color, stars beginning to make their appearance. Liza was so busy looking up at the sky and out at the ocean that she didn't notice the table and chairs sitting to her right until Ben walked over to them and pulled out a chair.

"Your seat, Ms. Hall."

Liza was too stunned to ask questions. Logically, she knew the table and chairs weren't a permanent feature of the cliff, but she also couldn't imagine Ben would go to this kind of trouble for her.

He ducked away from the table and reached behind a nearby tree, where Liza realized a battery-powered space heater was hiding. He brought it close to the table and kicked it on. Almost immediately, Liza felt the warmth.

Then, he went behind the tree again and pulled out a large wicker basket.

"We're having a picnic?" Liza asked, sounding more than a little dubious.

"In a sense." Ben opened the basket and pulled out a series of to-go containers, paper bags, and plastic containers. "I asked a few locals where all the best date spots are, and I knew there was a chance I'd only get one crack at this, so I decided to get all of their suggestions."

He continued pulling out containers, and Liza gaped at the growing mountain of food. "You brought a meal from every place they recommended?"

"And dessert." He pulled out a bag with *Romano's* printed on the side of a paper pastry bag that looked like the one Liza had gotten at The Roast for her biscotti the other morning, and a square box with a Good Stuff Cupcakes sticker holding it closed.

"How many people did you ask? This is enough food for ten people. Maybe more."

"How many people are in your book club?" he asked. "That's how many people I asked. Though, three of the women gave the same answer: Barb, Cheri, and Pam, I think."

That checks out, Liza thought, laughing to herself.

Ben went through each food item, letting Liza knew who had selected it. "Alma said her saloon, obviously, so I got a blooming onion from her for the appetizer, and she threw in a bottle of wine on the house. Georgia made me swear not to tell Alma, but she said she's never met a more talented chef than you, so she sent along some leftovers from a chicken and rice dish you made at the inn a couple nights ago. Stella said almond croissants from The Roast, and everyone said cannolis from Romano's were a must. Just for fun, I threw in a few slices of pizza from the gas station on the edge of town. I know what you're thinking, but it is truly incredible pizza. Shockingly good."

Liza studied the mass of food in front of her warily, trying to beat down the rush of emotions that threatened to rise up in her.

"Oh, and Georgia's son, Drew, said this is the best view in town. He lent me the table and chairs."

This was romantic—probably the most romantic thing anyone had ever done for Liza—and she did not know how to respond.

She'd thought being physically close to Ben would be difficult, but this? Liza did not know how to deal with the way he managed to climb inside of her rib cage and find direct access to her heart.

In her many years of marriage to Cliff, he'd never managed to understand that intentionality meant everything to her. Liza would rather have a piece of macaroni art that took him thirty hours to make than have him buy her the most expensive piece of jewelry.

Liza appreciated effort and thoughtfulness, and the fact that Ben had taken the time to ask people for recommendations, order all of the food, and set up the table, chairs, and heater beforehand was beyond anything she'd imagined for their date.

Liza didn't know how to not be affected by this.

"And don't worry about the food waste," he said, grabbing two plastic wineglasses out of the basket and filling them with the white wine

Alma had sent. "Georgia assured me anything you and I didn't want would be inhaled by Drew."

"Did Georgia help you plan this?" Liza hoped she had. That would make it easier to dispel the stars that had begun to form around Ben's head in her vision like a halo.

"She gave me the chicken and rice, like I said, and lent me the space heater from the inn." Ben held a hand to the side of his mouth even though no one else was around. "And between you and me, I think she likes you a lot. If this goes poorly, I might not have a room to return to at the end of the night."

Liza laughed, the first genuine one all night, and Ben's eyes widened in surprise. He hid it quickly and began unwrapping the food, his lips pressed together in his own hidden smile.

Thanks to the insulated liner Ben had wrapped around the hot items, the blooming onion was still warm when they cracked into it. The Khao Tom Gai was cold, but considering she'd made it herself, Liza didn't have much interest in eating it. Really, she wanted the gas station pizza.

"You're serious?" Ben asked, hand perched on the cardboard box like it was Pandora's Box, and he was afraid to open it. "I did not imagine you'd actually eat this. You're sure?"

"Should I not be? I thought you said it was good."

"It is!"

"Then, give me a slice." Liza held out her hand, and Ben opened the box and carefully pulled out a slice of meat lovers pizza.

The crust was hand tossed and golden, and long strings of cheese stretched between the slice and the rest of the pizza in the box. If she'd had no idea it came from a gas station, Liza would have thought the pizza came from a proper pizzeria.

Ben watched her with wide, impatient eyes as she bit off the end of the pizza slice.

Part of Liza wanted to hate it, but she couldn't.

"Oh my gosh." She covered her mouth with her hand and chewed, shaking her head. "How is this so good?"

"Right? It's insane. Sam told me it was the best pizza around, and I thought for sure I'd get food poisoning, but it's genuinely amazing."

"The crust is perfect. Somehow crunchy and chewy."

He shrugged. "It makes no sense. It tastes as good as the pizza I had in Italy that came out of thousand-degree brick ovens. I don't know, maybe there's a brick oven behind the gas station."

The delight Liza felt at how amazing the unconventional pizza was dampened at the mention of Ben's travels. If Ben noticed, he didn't say anything. Neither of them did. They both went back to eating quietly, occasionally pointing out ships far out on the water or remarking on the lovely evening.

The cannolis from Romano's were as amazing as everyone had said. Crunchy and creamy and sweet and balanced.

"I've got to add cannolis to my catering menu. These are incredible."

"Not in Willow Beach, though," Ben said. "If you stepped on Romano's cannoli game, you might end up sleeping with the fishes."

Liza barked out a surprised laugh. "I don't think the Italian mob has very strong ties to Willow Beach."

He shrugged. "Better safe than sorry. Stay in your own lane."

A sugar rush was creeping up on her, threatening a severe crash later, but Liza couldn't pass up the almond croissants Ben had brought. Apparently, Vivienne had broken into her frozen stash of croissants and baked these special for their date, which explained why they were still warm and fluffy on the inside. Croissants usually didn't keep long beyond twenty-four hours.

"This croissant is as big as my head, but I will eat the entire thing, and I'd like you not to judge me."

Ben held up his hands in surrender. "No judgment from me. Believe me, I know better than to get between a woman and her croissant."

Liza's face must have revealed the questions spinning in her mind because Ben leaned forward slightly, his mouth tipped in a smile. "I meant my daughter. She is a croissant fanatic. The number one fan, I think. I took her to Portland, Oregon, for her sixteenth birthday, and she stopped at every coffee shop we passed to get a croissant. Do you know how many coffee shops there are in that city?"

Ben kept talking, but Liza was stuck on one point.

Daughter.

"You have a daughter." A statement, not a question. Liza was using too much of her brain power processing to think of anything more profound to say.

"I do. She's twenty-six."

Liza did some quick math in her head. Three years after they broke up, Ben had gotten a woman pregnant. Was she his wife? His girlfriend? Neither? Liza wanted to ask, but it wasn't polite. Besides, it wasn't her business. Unless he was still married.

The possibility sank inside of her like a stone, weighing her down. Again, Ben seemed to be able to read her like her emotions were being projected on a jumbotron above her head.

"Her mom and I dated for a while, and we tried to make it work once our daughter was born, but it was better for Heather that we split up and focus on coparenting versus being a couple."

"Her name is Heather?"

"Heather Boyd." He smiled, like the mere sound of his daughter's name was his favorite song.

Liza let out a long string of curse words in her mind. Attractive, charming, romantic, and now, paternal? Ben was playing dirty. What kind of woman could resist that?

He pulled out his phone and showed Liza a picture. Ben was standing with a dark-haired girl who was the younger, feminine version of him —gorgeous, in other words—in front of a tall brick building that looked like a college dorm. They both had on UMass Boston shirts.

"She's beautiful," Liza said. "My niece goes to UMass Boston, too. She's getting a business degree so she can become my full-time partner and at least one of us will have an education."

"They might know each other, then. That's what Heather is studying, too."

"Does she know what she wants to do with it yet?"

"She wants to be settled, unlike her old man." He smiled, but Liza sensed a bit of self-doubt there. Perhaps hurt, even. "I've bounced around from job to job for most of my life. Now, I'm four books into a mystery series that pays enough in royalties for me to feed myself, and I use my experience as a draftsman to find freelance work to cover everything else. I'm happy with it, but Heather wants something more conventional."

Liza blinked. "You wrote a book?"

"Four of them," he said, holding up four fingers. "I published with an indie press you've never heard of, I'm sure."

"Still," she said, shaking her head. "You're a published writer. I had no idea."

And a father, she thought, mentally adding to the list. She'd avoided looking up where Ben was for fear she'd find something she didn't want to see. Really, it felt like a lose-lose situation. If she found out he was married and happy and successful, she'd resent him, and if he was miserable, she'd feel guilty. Or, she'd feel smug and like he'd received his just desserts, and then she'd feel guilty for feeling *that* way. There was no way to win, so Liza avoided all news of him.

Again, that same expression of hurt or...something crossed his face, but he hid it well. "Most people don't. I don't exactly advertise it – that's the publisher's job. Let's talk about something other than me."

"I think that would be me," Liza said, playfully raising her hand. "That's usually how conversations on a date go."

It was growing dark and the battery-operated candle in the middle of the table didn't let off much light, but Liza thought she saw a flush rise in Ben's cheeks. "Apparently, I was the only one of us who utilized the power of the internet."

Liza frowned. "What?"

"I looked you up."

Why hadn't that possibility occurred to her? Liza had made the choice not to look Ben up, but she'd never considered that he'd type her name into a search bar.

"When? I can't imagine you found anything too interesting. My catering website, probably?"

He laughed nervously. "Now I really feel like we should talk about something else."

"Why?"

His expression turned serious, and he met her eyes over the flickering candle. "Because yours was the first name I typed into every new form of social media over the years. Myspace, Facebook, Twitter, Instagram. It took me a while to learn you'd gotten married because you didn't change your maiden name and there wasn't a spouse listed on your Facebook."

"Cliff thought social media was a waste of time," Liza said, her voice barely above a whisper.

Ben nodded and lowered his head, unfolding and refolding the napkin in his lap. Finally, he looked up at her from under heavy brows. "I noticed a few years ago that your ring wasn't in any of your photos. And since you're here with me, I assume Cliff isn't in the picture anymore?"

Was she here with him? The way he said it made Liza's insides tingle. It filled her with equal parts giddiness and dread. What was she getting herself into?

"He filed for divorce a few years ago."

"What an idiot." Ben spoke so softly Liza wasn't even sure if she was supposed to have heard him, so she didn't say anything. He looked at the watch on his wrist and sighed. "It's about time to pack up and head back if I'm going to get you home by curfew."

～

Ben walked around the car and opened Liza's door. He handed her a plastic bag filled with the other almond croissant, the rest of the cannolis, and the pizza.

"I'm keeping the chicken and rice," he said. "I have a feeling Georgia's right and it will be better than anything else we had tonight."

Liza's stomach was in such a knot she couldn't imagine ever eating again.

How had she forgotten about the end of the date? Before he'd arrived, she'd been focused on sitting in the car with him and making small talk, but she hadn't given any consideration to the end of the night.

Honestly, it was because she partly imagined they'd be so sick of each other after three hours that she'd jump out of his still-moving car the moment the cottage came into view and run inside.

But Ben was walking her to the front door, and Liza didn't know what she was going to do. Worse, she didn't know what she wanted to do.

Ben stood behind her quietly as she fumbled in her purse for her keys. Liza could feel the warmth of him like a physical touch.

When she finally got the door unlocked, she considered just walking inside and waving from the safety of the other side of the threshold, but instead, she turned around.

He was standing closer than she thought. Closer than they'd been in a long time.

Liza had to look up to see his face.

"So, was it horrible?" he asked, smirking. "As bad as you remember?"

"Dates with you were never bad."

He shoved his hands in his pockets and rocked on his heels. "Does that mean you'd be willing to do this again?"

Willing? Yes.

Liza was willing to do lots of things she shouldn't, seeing Ben again being one of them.

A cold wind blew and Liza shivered. "I'd consider it," she said quietly.

Ben bit the corner of his lip and took a microscopic step forward. "Is there anything I can do to make you certain?"

He's going to kiss me, Liza thought.

She knew she shouldn't. Kissing Ben would seal her fate. This date was supposed to be proof that she didn't have any feelings for him, but things had not gone at all to plan. Despite every intention not to, Liza enjoyed herself. He was just as thoughtful and fun and charming as he had been thirty years ago. Plus, he'd kept up with her over the years.

Liza didn't know what that meant exactly, but she knew it meant he'd thought about her.

Did he have regrets? Did he want to fix his mistake from all those years ago? Did he want a second chance?

With every passing second, the kiss Liza was expecting took on more and more meaning, but Liza also grew more and more impatient for it. She felt herself arch towards him, expectant.

But Ben didn't kiss her. He didn't even try.

"How about we discuss it over breakfast tomorrow?"

"What?" Liza asked, slightly dazed.

"It's not a date, don't worry. It will be like a post-game analysis, and then you can decide whether we should go on another real date."

"An analysis?"

"Yes, exactly," he said. "But analyzing on an empty stomach is impossible, so I'll grab coffee for us in the morning and, if it suits you, you can make pancakes. We can reconvene at 8 a.m.?"

Liza knew what he was doing, but she couldn't resist. She wanted to spend more time with him, but she also needed twelve hours to consider all of the implications. So, it seemed like the perfect plan.

"Okay. I'll see you in the morning."

Ben couldn't hide his glee. He beamed and bounced on his toes. "Great. I'll see you then."

He waited to leave until she went inside, but Liza waited until he'd driven away to stop looking through the peephole.

What had she gotten herself into?

15

"What are you doing up so early?" Liza asked as soon as she answered her phone.

She'd been up for two hours, showering, primping, and making a giant stack of fluffy pancakes, but Angela didn't usually wake up before nine on any day she didn't have to. And even when she did, she didn't seem to gain the full function of her mental faculties until ten in the morning or later, but it wasn't even seven thirty yet.

"Calling to see how you're doing," she said. "You haven't called or texted in days, and I was starting to get worried you actually did get murdered in that cottage."

"I didn't get murdered, but I did almost drown."

"What?!"

Liza related the story of the burst pipe to Angela, telling her about going to the inn for a room and, instead, finding Ben.

"Ben?" Angela asked, no small amount of interest in her voice. "Pray tell, who is Ben?"

"He's the brother of the client I'm catering for, Stacy Boyd. He's the bro of honor in the wedding, and he's staying at the inn in town to help iron out wedding details. He came over to the house and helped turn off the water and clean up the mess. Without him, I'd be underwater and homeless."

"Well, that was generous of him. I don't know many strangers who would be so willing to help someone in the middle of the night like that. He must be a saint."

"Well..." Liza had been debating telling Angela about Ben for a couple days now. Unlike Dora, Angela could be an objective third party. She didn't know Ben. She knew nothing about Liza and Ben's history. Plus, Angela was the one who'd sent Liza to Willow Beach to focus on her future. Those three things converged to make her the person most likely to give Liza an honest, sincere answer of how to move forward with Ben.

"Okay, I'm sensing there's a lot more to this story," Angela said. "You have to tell me. It's early, and the only thing that energizes me more than caffeine is juicy gossip."

"It's not juicy gossip, but there is more to the story. You see, I actually know Ben. We used to...date."

Angela screamed on the other end of the phone, forcing Liza to pull it away from her ear.

"What? I had no idea. How crazy is that?"

"Crazy," Liza agreed. "It was a very long time ago, and I tried to keep my distance, but he seems interested in reconnecting, and...I don't know. I'm not so sure it's a terrible idea."

"Of course, it's not," Angela said. "I sent you to Willow Beach to relax and start fresh, and there is no better way to start fresh than with a handsome man."

"How do you know he's handsome? What if he's hideous? Does that change your opinion?"

"I doubt you'd ever date anyone who is hideous. Not to say you're shallow, but birds of a feather usually flock together where things like this are concerned, and you're a total catch, Aunt Liza."

"Okay, but dating an ex isn't exactly a fresh start, is it?"

"It can be!" Angela argued. "It totally can be. Especially after thirty years. You are both different people than you were back then. It's totally different."

Liza frowned. "How do you know it's been thirty years?"

There was a brief pause. "I don't know. I just assumed. You and Uncle Cliff were together for twenty years, and I'm twenty-six, and I don't remember seeing any other men in our old pictures. I assumed you dated him before I was born."

"I was younger than you when we dated," Liza said. "I can't believe it has been that long. Especially since he is so similar. Still so charming and thoughtful, and still perfectly capable of getting under my skin and driving me bananas."

Angela laughed. "Aunt Liza, you're *into* this guy. I can totally hear it in your voice. You like him!"

Liza smiled and flipped a pancake in the skillet. "You don't think I'm being foolish? What if this is just a rebound after my divorce?"

"What if it is? Does it matter? You deserve to be happy, and if this guy makes you happy, you should go for it. Fate has spoken."

Fate. There was that word again.

Could this be fate?

Liza had given up hope that the universe had a grander plan for her life, but suddenly, she wondered if she wasn't living a real-life romance novel. Just like the book the book club was reading, she and

Ben were crossing paths decades later, after Liza's divorce and when she was on a quest to start over.

"He has a daughter. She goes to UMass Boston. Her name is Heather Boyd."

Angela hummed in thought. "Maybe I've heard that name. I'm not sure. I'll have to keep an eye out for her. Especially since we might be cousins-in-law some day!"

"I don't think that's a thing," Liza laughed. "And you're definitely getting ahead of yourself. "We've only gone on one date."

"Do you have a second one planned?"

Liza's cheeks flushed. "He'll be here in fifteen minutes. We're having breakfast."

Angela squealed. "Uncle Ben and Aunt Liza. I like the sound of that."

Liza laughed and bid Angela farewell. She was glad to have her niece's blessing, but she didn't need that thought rolling around in her head when Ben arrived. Yes, she was excited. Yes, she wanted to see him. Yes, she liked spending time with him.

But she wasn't going to get ahead of herself.

Liza had already made the mistake of planning for a future with Ben, and she wasn't going to let herself be hurt so easily a second time. If they were going to try this again, she was going to guard her heart.

~

Ben swore he was coming over to analyze their date the night before, but after five minutes of extolling their natural chemistry and how much fun they had together, Ben seemed content to schedule a second date.

Liza was content, too.

Though, the way she felt with Ben as the days passed was far more than contentment.

"Contented" was the way her marriage had felt. She and Cliff weren't happy, but they weren't miserable, which is why they'd stayed married for so long. It was harder to leave a situation that wasn't working when you were comfortable.

With Ben, however, everything felt exciting. Normal things, like watching a movie on the couch, walking down Main Street for coffee, and going to the grocery store for milk, were fun. Ben teased Liza for talking through scenes in a movie and then asking him to explain what was going on five minutes later. He'd go into The Roast to get them both coffees, and come out with a cake pop held behind his back for Liza, knowing she wanted one even though she didn't ask. And when a good song came on over the speakers in the grocery store, Ben used a zucchini as a microphone and put on a lip-syncing performance for the ages, earning cheers from nearby customers.

Ben brought out a side of Liza she'd left behind long ago. He helped her see the beauty in ordinary things. He picked dandelions from cracks in the concrete and presented them to her like the most expensive bouquet, and Liza took them home to press between the pages of books.

"When are you leaving Willow Beach?" They were sitting on Liza's front porch under a blanket, mugs of steaming tea in their hands. "Will you stay until your sister's wedding or—"

"Honestly, I don't have anywhere to return to," Ben said. "I was living in Quincy, but I was starting to feel restless, so I sold my apartment and traveled for a bit. Freelancing means I can work from anywhere. Then, Stacy got engaged and needed my help, so, here I am."

"You're kind of a nomad."

Ben shrugged. "After Heather left for college, there wasn't a need to stay put in one place. I've stayed in hotels, taken over leases for a few months at a time, and even lived in a camper for six months. As long as I have a place nearby with a reliable internet connection, I can make money anywhere. So, I can stay in Willow Beach as long as you want."

"It's not up to me," Liza said quickly. "I'm not going to force you to stay put anywhere if you don't want to."

Ben smiled and leaned closer, nudging her shoulder with his. "That's just it, Liza. You don't need to force me to stay. I'll stay so long as you don't force me to go."

They'd been together for days on end, and Ben still hadn't tried to kiss her. Not once.

But sitting with him on the porch swing while he asked her not to make him leave felt much more intimate.

$\sim$

In the days leading up to the wedding, Ben turned Liza's cottage into wedding headquarters. Every morning, he'd come over with coffee, occasionally croissants, and would make calls and arrangements from her kitchen table. Liza worked on making pastry dough for the mini beef Wellingtons and checking and double-checking her supplies to ensure she had everything she needed. Since she didn't have her industrial kitchen, she'd have to make a lot of things ahead of time.

Spending so much time together, Liza kept expecting Ben to get sick of her. To want some space. To show signs of feeling trapped or tied down. But he didn't.

He showed up earlier every day, knocking on the door a few times before Liza had even dried her hair, and he stayed until Liza was ready to go to bed.

It took Liza back to her days as a waitress at the bar and grill, working while Ben sat at a table, waiting for her shift to end.

It felt nice, but she couldn't entirely keep away the doubts.

She hadn't noticed any signs of him pulling away back then, either. In the days before he broke up with her, he'd been just as sweet and charming and thoughtful as ever.

What had Liza missed?

Had she done something to push him away? Or had he simply grown bored with her?

Most importantly, would it happen again?

The questions sat unspoken between them, but Liza decided they would wait until after the wedding. Neither of them had the time to dive into them now. Besides, Liza wasn't sure she wanted to know the answer. She wanted to live in this bubble of bliss for as long as possible before reality had a chance to pop it.

16

Liza let out a string of curses that would have made her mother call their pastor, but cursing had never been more appropriate.

Her oven was broken.

Or, rather, Mrs. Albertson's twenty-year-old gas oven was broken.

Liza had noticed the oven was in less than ideal condition when she arrived, but it cooked food remarkably evenly. Until it didn't.

Now, it was the day of Stacy and Jonathan's wedding, and Liza didn't have an oven.

"What do I do?" she mumbled, pulling trays of food out of the cold oven and setting them on the counter.

It was too late to call a repairman and far too late to order a new oven. Liza needed a working oven *now*.

As she thought through all of her options, her phone rang. It was a number she didn't recognize, but she answered it, anyway.

"Hey, Liza." Georgia Baldwin's voice came over the phone line, and Liza felt a weight life off her shoulders. "The inn is all abuzz with

Stacy's wedding guests getting ready for the big day, but none of them need my help. So, I thought I'd call and see if you needed anything. I hate feeling useless."

"Are you an angel? Or a mind reader?"

Georgia laughed. "No, but I take it you need some help?"

"You have no idea." Liza explained that she had countless trays of food ready to be put in an oven that was no longer working.

"Well that I can help with. Breakfast is over, so my kitchen is free to use the rest of the day. Bring your stuff over here and turn this place into your personal kitchen. I'll help or stay out of your way, whatever you need."

"Georgia Baldwin, you're a saint."

Georgia laughed. "You won't be saying that when I steal bites of your cooking all day."

"That's a fair price to pay for you saving my behind today."

Liza loaded up her Tupperware containers, supplies, and wedding outfit in Mrs. Albertson's car and drove over to the inn as fast as she could.

As soon as she pulled up, Ben walked out the side door. He was wearing suit pants with a white button-down tucked in, but no jacket. His hair was mussed, strands falling over his forehead, and he was in such a hurry to get down the stairs and to his car that he didn't see Liza right away.

When he did notice her, he stopped short and blinked. "Liza? What are you doing here? Not that I'm not happy to see you, I just...I didn't expect to see you." He sighed and walked towards her, pulling her in for a hug. "I'm happy to see you."

They'd sat close and snuggled under blankets and held hands, but they hadn't hugged yet, and Liza felt it down to her toes. The stress she felt that morning seemed suddenly more bearable, like Ben absorbed some of it for her.

"I'm happy to see you, too," she said. "I've had a morning."

"That makes two of us. What happened to you?"

"My oven broke. I'm here to use Georgia's. What happened to you?"

"The sole of my shoe came off. I'm running out to buy super glue right now before Stacy finds out. Jonathan's flight was delayed, so he isn't going to get into town for a few more hours, and Stacy is freaking out that he'll miss the wedding."

Liza looked down and realized he had on white sneakers with his suit pants instead of dress shoes.

"Wow, okay. So, I should probably hide in the kitchen in hopes she doesn't find out about my oven situation?" Liza asked. "It sounds like she doesn't need the extra stress."

Ben laid a hand on her shoulder. "If you don't mind, that might be best."

She waved him away. "Of course not. My job is to make the bride's day easier. As soon as my supplies are inside, I won't need to leave, anyway. Just keep Stacy away from the kitchen."

Ben ran a hand through his hair, smoothing it down slightly. "Are weddings always this stressful?"

Liza didn't know if he was asking her about her own wedding or her experience working at other people's weddings. "It depends on a lot of different things. Not always."

"Was yours?"

Aside from their first date, they hadn't really discussed Cliff or made any mention of him, so Liza had begun to feel like the topic was off-limits. Though, of course it wasn't. How could twenty years of her life be off-limits?

Liza wondered for a second if she should lie, but she didn't see the point. Ben knew how things had ended with her and Cliff. There wasn't any need to be jealous.

She shook her head. "No, it was perfect. It was a wonderful day."

He gave her a small smile. "I bet you were a beautiful bride."

With that, they parted ways, Ben off to buy super glue, and Liza to the kitchen.

As soon as she walked in, Georgia raised her hands in the air like she was in a cooking competition and the host had just called time.

"Done," she said, twirling a rag in the air. "I just speed-cleaned the kitchen and preheated the oven to three fifty for you. Is there anything else I can do?"

"You've already done enough." Liza set a stack of Tupperware containers on the island. "You are so generous to let me use your kitchen. I'll clean up after myself and make sure everything is back where it belongs."

"Please," Georgia said, chuckling to herself. "Nothing is ever back where it belongs with this kitchen. I'm a very disorganized cook, which is why I pulled things out for you. Use whatever you need and make as big of a mess as you want. I'm happy to have you here."

Liza put trays in the oven while she wrapped and pinned bacon around scallops, chopped vegetables, and seasoned and rolled meatballs for the Italian wedding soup. As she worked, the stress of the morning began to fade away. Cooking had always worked like that for Liza.

There were so many problems in the world—so many issues she couldn't solve—but she could turn a pile of raw ingredients into a delicious meal. She could follow a recipe step by step and end up with a delicious final product. Cooking provided a sense of order in the disorder of life, and Liza took full solace in that feeling while preparing for Stacy's wedding.

Once everything was prepped and baking, all Liza had to do was start the soup.

Except, she didn't have her containers of stock. She'd made fresh chicken stock two days earlier, letting it simmer on the stove for twenty-four hours to extract every last drop of flavor. Now, it was nowhere to be found.

"Don't panic," she said out loud to herself. The stock was probably in the car. It was cold enough outside that a few hours in the car wouldn't have ruined it. Everything was fine.

As soon as Liza opened the passenger side door, the overwhelming smell of chicken hit her, and her heart sank.

Mrs. Albertson's car hadn't smelled wonderful to begin with. It was dusty and old and remnants of musty floral perfume clung to the upholstery, but it certainly hadn't smelled like chicken. And even with chicken stock in the car, it shouldn't smell this strongly. Liza used restaurant-quality plasticware to transport her food. It was airtight.

She reached down and pressed her hand into the floor mat and fragrant liquid bubbled up around her fingers.

Chicken stock.

Tears welled in her eyes almost instantly. As she walked around to open the hatchback, she blinked away the emotion.

Everything will be fine. Everything will be fine. Everything will be fine.

She opened the hatch, and it was like a bloodbath, only if the blood was chicken stock.

The large cylindrical plastic container she'd put the broth in had a crack in it, and all of the stock had leaked out while it sat in the trunk.

Liza remembered grabbing the container from the fridge and hearing a plastic snapping noise, but she'd thought it had been the lid shifting. Then, after putting the container in the car, her hand had been slightly wet, but she'd thought it was condensation or some spilled chicken stock that had gathered around the bottom of the container.

She never checked the container for cracks. She never even considered it.

Now, her stock for the soup was gone and—

Her eyes caught on the garment bag resting on the floor of the trunk, and a sob caught in her throat.

The bag had been hanging on a hook from the ceiling, but when she reached over the back seat to grab the stock pot from the trunk, the dress had fallen, and Liza had never picked it up.

She lunged for it and lifted it into the air, and rivulets of chicken stock washed down the front. She prayed that the bag was waterproof, but as soon as she unzipped it, she could see that the satiny dress fabric had taken on a darker color. She threw the sodden garment in the trunk and, for the second time that day, cursed.

"Uh-oh."

Liza spun around and saw Stella Pierce standing behind her, a worried look on her face. "Is everything okay?"

Worse things happened in the world every day, Liza knew that. Natural disasters, starving people, injustice, murder. Yet, none of those things were happening to her right now. *This* was happening, and she'd give anything for it to stop.

She opened her mouth to answer Stella, but her emotions overwhelmed her, and she began to cry. Truly and earnestly.

"Oh, honey." Stella wrapped an arm around Liza's shoulders and led her away from the car. "We'll fix this. Don't worry."

Stella took Liza inside, and Georgia was standing at the island, one of the mini beef Wellingtons in her hand. She dropped it on the tray as soon as they walked in, looking guilty. "I was just looking."

"We don't have time for your lies, Georgia. Liza is in crisis."

Georgia shifted into full-on caregiver mode in an instant. Her expression softened, and she rounded the island and grabbed Liza's elbow, turning her so they were face-to-face. "What's going on, dear?"

Liza had regained control of her tears, at least, and relayed her tale of the ruined dress and spilled stock.

"I have cartons of chicken stock in the pantry," Georgia said, gesturing for Stella to go and grab them. "They aren't going to be nearly as good as yours, I'm sure, but to be honest, none of the plebeians at this wedding will know the difference."

Liza almost laughed, despite everything. "I don't think they'd appreciate being called that."

"Well, you didn't serve them breakfast this morning," Georgia whispered. "The bride's family complimented the cappuccinos I made them from instant powder mix. The groom's family didn't touch the stuff, but then again, Italians know a thing or two about coffee. None of them are going to know you used a boxed stock for your soup, I promise."

Stella set three boxes of stock on the counter and waved her hands in the air like she was a model on a game show revealing a prize.

"And I can help with the dress," Stella said. "You and I look to be around the same size. I'll run to my house, grab you a few options, and be back in a jiffy."

"My shoes were back there too," Liza said, wiping her sleeve across her nose, feeling like a toddler. "I only brought the one pair of heels, and my feet are bigger than most women's. It's hard for me to find shoes."

Georgia and Stella looked at each other and, at the same time, said, "Alma."

"Everything is bigger in Texas, including Alma's shoe size," Georgia laughed. "She wears a ten. Will that work for you?"

Liza was a nine and a half, but she'd take what she could get right now. Even if it meant wearing cowboy boots with a borrowed dress.

"Yeah, I think that will work."

Georgia spun around and grabbed a paper towel and then handed it to Liza, giving her a kind smile. "Blow your nose, wash your hands, and make some soup. We'll take care of the rest."

Liza had never wanted to hug a person more in her life. But, in her snotty, tear-stained state, she figured Georgia wouldn't appreciate it. So, she nodded, followed Georgia's directions, and got back to work.

~

By the time the soup was simmering on the stove, Liza felt embarrassed for her freak-out. She'd been doing this job for years, and she'd never had a meltdown like that before. Usually, she was the pinnacle of calm, cool, and collected. This was so unlike her.

Just as Liza was undoing her apron, Stella walked into the kitchen. "Perfect timing. Are you ready to see your options?"

Liza followed Stella down a hallway and into a small office. Georgia was inside with a steamer, getting rid of the wrinkles on three dresses hanging from the accordion-style doors of a closet.

"All of the rooms upstairs are full, and Stacy is in the sunroom with her bridesmaids, so you get the office," Georgia said, standing back. "What do you think?"

All three of the dresses were beautiful—long gowns in jewel tones— but Liza's eyes caught on the maroon number hanging on the end. It was a maroon wrap dress with flowing sleeves and a high slit up the side. It was modest, yet sexy, and Liza couldn't help but reach out and touch it.

"That one is my favorite too," Stella said, beaming. "Georgia's daughters actually helped me pick it out. If Tasha wasn't busy prepping to sing at the wedding, I would have called her to help you get ready. She's so much better at it than me."

"Nonsense," Liza said, pulling the dress down from the hanger. "You're wonderful at this. I love this dress so much more than the one I was planning to wear."

Georgia bent down and lifted a pair of nude strappy heels. "Oh, and these are from Alma. She said you can keep them if you want. She's intimidating enough without adding another four inches of height."

Once again, Liza felt tears burning at the backs of her eyelids. But this time, it wasn't out of stress or feeling overwhelmed. It was gratitude.

These people barely knew her, but they had jumped into action at the first sign of trouble, and Liza didn't know if she could ever thank them for that.

"No more tears," Stella said with a stern finger.

"Yeah, Melanie will be here in five minutes to do your makeup, and we don't want puffy eyes." Georgia patted Liza on the back, and then she and Stella left the room so Liza could change.

As soon as Liza put on the dress, she knew what was different about today compared to other weddings. It hit her all at once, and it was so obvious she almost laughed.

Ben.

Ben was different.

Liza was catering his sister's wedding, and she was wearing a dress that he would see her in.

She wanted to impress him, even though he'd never once made her feel like she needed to earn his approval. Liza wanted to wow him and his family with her food, and she wanted to wow him with her appearance, and the momentary thought that all of that was lost had broken her heart.

Seeing herself in this maroon wrap dress, however, mended it back together.

Liza looked awesome.

There was a knock at the door, and then Melanie walked in and whistled. "You look stunning."

Speaking of stunning, Melanie looked gorgeous. She had on a pair of dark gray high-waisted trousers with cropped ankles, a billowy green blouse, and gold high heels with straps around her ankles. The outfit, paired with her peaches and cream complexion and her strawberry-blonde hair falling in beach waves around her face, made her look like a model fresh from the pages of a fashion magazine.

"Me? Look at you. You're beautiful."

"Thank you," she said. "This is the first formal event I get to attend with Colin, so I wanted to make the most of it. I assume that's why I'm here to help you, as well? Mom told me you've been spending a lot of time with a certain guest at the inn."

Liza flushed. "Perhaps."

Melanie laid her makeup bag open on the desk and winked. "Good for you. He's a babe."

"He is, isn't he?" Liza smiled.

"Yes, but you are no slouch yourself, Liza." Melanie pulled out a powder brush as large as her face and turned to Liza. "Ben is going to lose his mind when he sees you."

≈

Liza loved weddings.

Over the years, she'd met people who worked in the industry and hated them. They would complain about the bride being overbearing and the families being ungrateful. They'd moan about all of the limits being placed on their creativity and talent.

And sure, some of that was true. Liza had dealt with brides who thought they knew best despite what Liza said. She'd worked with families who wanted a discount because the dinner wasn't piping hot after an hour-long delay when the groom got cold feet.

However, on the whole, Liza was at a wedding to make the bride and groom's dreams come true. Food wasn't the most important part of the day, Liza knew, but it played a role, and Liza was honored every time a bride chose to eat Liza's food on her wedding day.

More than that, though, weddings were beautiful.

Liza loved seeing the way Jonathan shifted nervously on the altar as the bridal party walked down the aisle. (She also loved seeing Ben walk down the aisle, his shoe glued together, and his hair gelled down into handsome, picture-perfect obedience.) Then, Stacy walked in.

The audience rose, Jonathan's fidgeting stopped, and it was as though nothing else in the whole world mattered except for the two of them.

Which, in that moment, was true.

Liza always felt like time stopped during a wedding, like everything that was good about the world and life and humanity came together to create a perfect moment in time.

Unfortunately, being the caterer meant Liza didn't often get to sit in on the ceremonies. When she did, she sat in the back and then ducked out before the vows, as she did for Stacy and Jonathan's wedding. Then, while the bridal party and families were busy being photographed, Liza got to work.

She donned an apron over Stella's wrap dress, heated everything through and filled chafing dishes, and double-checked the place settings. The time between the ceremony and the reception was a mad dash of last-minute fixes and prep, but it was always worth it when guests arrived and began to eat.

Liza was so busy ladling out soup into bowls and making sure the chafing dishes were refilled that she didn't even see when Ben went through the food line, but from what little she overheard from the guests closest to the kitchen, her food was a hit.

After service, while the bride and groom were cutting the cake, Liza made herself a plate and sat down in the kitchen to eat. Her legs were so tired she actually sighed with relief.

Kate, from Good Stuff Cupcakes, joined her.

"These mini beef Wellingtons are amazing," she said. "I love eating small versions of big foods. Which, now that I think about it, is probably why I love making cupcakes."

"Did you just make that connection?"

"Believe it or not, I did," Katie laughed. She leaned forward and peeked through the partially opened kitchen door. "People are lining up to eat cake. It looks like our jobs are done for the day. Are you going to stick around?"

"Yeah, I'm kind of..." Liza paused, unsure how to explain. "I'm here with the brother of the bride."

Katie snapped her attention to Liza, eyes wide. "Ben? Girl, good for you. I met him this morning when I dropped off the cake, and he is a dreamboat. And so nice."

Liza blushed, but before she could formulate a response, the man himself walked into the kitchen. "Hey, I hope I'm not interrupting, but I wondered if you were—"

Ben's eyes fell on Liza and went wide. He stopped speaking for a moment, and Liza was conscious of the fact that she was sitting on a counter with a plate of food in her lap and a napkin tucked into the collar of her dress.

Quickly, she set aside her plate, pulled the napkin from around her neck, and stood up.

Ben's eyes went even wider as he looked Liza up and down.

"Did you lose your train of thought?" Katie asked, stifling a laugh.

Ben swallowed. "The dancing is about to start, and I wondered if you'd be done in here in time to dance with me."

"She's done," Katie said, nudging the back of Liza's leg.

Liza looked at the mountain of dishes in the sink. "Are you sure? I can help with—"

"Nothing," Katie finished. "I was invited to the wedding as a courtesy. I don't know anyone. I'd be happy to wash some dishes while you enjoy yourself. Go, go."

Liza thanked Katie and then followed Ben out into the main reception hall.

Coming out from behind the food line, Liza really took in the splendor of the place for the first time.

The reception hall was a renovated barn not far from Georgia's inn, which was why all of the wedding party got ready there. String lights hung from the rafters, giving the room a magical glow, and the flowers and candles and flowing tablecloths set the mood. It was an understated, gorgeous wedding.

"Everything looks so beautiful," Liza said.

Suddenly, Ben grabbed her hand and pulled her into him smoothly. He wrapped a hand around her lower back and began to sway along with the music. "The decorations are fine. *You*, however, are gorgeous."

"You clean up pretty well yourself." Liza smoothed a hand down his lapel. "You're very fashionable."

"Are you surprised?"

Liza thought about it for a moment. "Honestly? Kind of. You were always handsome, but when I knew you, you wore pleated jeans and neon windbreakers."

"Hey! Don't blame me for the nineties. I was fashionable then, and I'm fashionable now." Ben spun Liza out and twirled her in a circle before pulling her close again. "But you've always been timeless. The most beautiful woman I've ever known."

Liza's heart swelled in her chest. She felt like she was floating, and it wasn't just because Ben was such a good dancer. With the romantic music, the dim lights, and the warmth in the air, it felt like the perfect moment. As hesitant as Liza was to admit it, it felt like fate.

Yet, a small voice in the back of her mind brought her back down to reality.

Liza loved weddings, but she was also aware that it was easy to get swept up in the romance and the grandeur. It was easy to forget that, like Cinderella, the clock would strike midnight and the magic would fade.

How much of what Ben was saying was because he was lost in the moment? How much of it was because he'd just sat through an hour-long ceremony where his sister pledged her love to another? Liza didn't want to hand over yet another piece of her heart only for it to be shattered because Ben wasn't as serious about her as she thought.

After all, Liza had heard compliments from Ben before.

Liza had told herself all week that she'd wait until after the wedding to have any sort of serious conversation with Ben, but dancing with him felt so good, and she was becoming more and more convinced with every second that fate had brought them back together, so she had to ask him now.

The walls she'd built around her heart were tumbling down, and if she didn't ask now, she'd be at serious risk of being heartbroken all over again.

Ben tucked a lock of Liza's hair behind her ear and frowned. "You have your serious face on. What is it?"

Liza looked into his green eyes as she gathered the courage to ask the question she'd been too afraid to voice for thirty years.

"Why did you leave me?"

17

Thirty Years Earlier

Liza waited for Ben to show up at the bar and grill after his shift ended at the bakery, but an hour passed, and he still hadn't showed.

It wasn't entirely unusual. Some days, he was too busy to come in and sit with her while she closed, but he usually told her about it beforehand. Plus, even if he couldn't make it the entire time, he almost always showed up to walk her across the dark parking lot to her car.

As Liza worked, she worried about him. Was he hurt? Sick? Had there been a family emergency?

She told herself she was probably overreacting. And when Ben showed up twenty minutes before closing time, she felt ridiculous.

"What a relief," Dora said, bumping Liza with her hip as she passed. "I was certain you were right, and he'd fallen into a coal mine."

Liza laughed. "Shut up."

All the girls at work told Liza she was spoiled, and now she knew they were right. Dora's last boyfriend had disappeared for an entire weekend one time with no explanation. Yet, Liza freaked out when Ben didn't show up to sit with her at work.

"Can I get you anything, sir?" Liza crooned, leaning over his shoulder to kiss him on the cheek.

He gave her a small smile and shook his head. "I'm fine."

The uneasy feeling she'd had earlier came back, but in a much smaller capacity. "You were late. I was worried you'd been kidnapped for a second."

"I got busy."

He kept his eyes on the table or trained on the television above the bar, and Liza felt the urge to grab his chin and turn his face to her. To force him to look at her.

"Sure, I get it," she said. "I'm not mad. I was just saying."

"Looks like someone wants their check." He tipped his head towards a table by the door where a man was waving his finger in the air. The guest had been waving Liza down for the last hour, requesting condiments the bar didn't have and asking her for refills when his glass was still half-full.

Liza wanted to ask Ben what was wrong, if something had happened, why he seemed so reserved, but she decided it could all wait until the guests were gone.

Usually, when Liza would walk by Ben's table, he'd whistle or wink or do something to acknowledge her, but he barely even looked at her.

In the last fifteen minutes of her shift, a knot began to form in Liza's stomach.

Then, the guests left and she and her coworkers began cleaning, and Ben stayed where he was in the corner of the room. He didn't come up to the bar while she washed glasses or wiped down the counter. He didn't play music in the jukebox for everyone or entertain her coworkers with jokes.

It felt like staring up at the sky, waiting for the asteroid to appear.

Liza knew something was wrong, she just didn't know what.

As far as she knew, she and Ben weren't in a fight. He'd come by her apartment the day before, and he'd seemed fine then. What had changed?

By the time the kitchen crew left and Liza dismissed the rest of the waitresses, letting them know she'd lock up, her chest was tight with anxiety of what was to come.

Even still, she didn't expect what was going to happen next.

"I'm about to lock up," she said, waving Ben out of the corner where he'd been hiding. "We didn't get much of a chance to talk. Do you want to go back to my place?"

Ben stood up and shoved his hands in his pockets. "Actually, I have to get going."

"Well, it was nice of you to wait this long just to walk me to my car. Maybe we can see each other tomorrow?"

Ben held open the door for Liza, and she walked outside into the cold. It had been almost a year since they'd kissed in the snow, and Liza could smell frost in the air.

"I can't. I have to go."

Liza turned to him, frowning. "What does that mean? Do you have to leave town or something?"

He shuffled his feet back and forth, and Liza couldn't remember a time she'd ever seen him so fidgety. Ben always oozed confidence and grace, but the man before her was nervous, itching to get away.

"I enlisted in the navy. I leave for boot camp tomorrow."

A sharp wind blew, but Liza had chills for another reason. She shook her head. "I don't...I don't understand. When did you enlist? How are you leaving tomorrow? That's so fast—"

"I enlisted a month ago. I wanted to tell you, but I didn't know how."

"How about, *'I'm going to boot camp'*?" Liza spat, feeling heat rising in her cheeks and tears burning in her eyes. "Or *'Hey, Liza, I enlisted in the navy.'* Both are great options. Anything would have been better than dropping it on me like this. I don't have any time to prepare. I would have taken time off work so we could be together. I wouldn't have spent our last night together working."

Ben lowered his head. "I thought it would be easier if we didn't spend too much time together."

This didn't make any sense. Liza knew she was being bombarded with bad information, so her ability to process was slower than normal, but why wouldn't Ben want to spend time with her? How would avoiding her make a long-distance relationship easier?

"How long is boot camp? Do you know where you'll be stationed afterward? Can you make phone calls or send letters? Surely, you can, right? It's not like you're going off to war."

Ben shifted his feet again, looking down at the ground.

Liza felt sick. "You're going off to war."

"That was the idea, yeah."

"Why didn't you tell me?" Her voice cracked. Liza wanted to stay strong. She wanted Ben to know she supported him, but this was too much all at once. She needed time to digest. To plan. To prepare.

He looked up at her, and his usually bright green eyes were dull and distant. It was almost like he'd already left.

"I wanted to delay the inevitable."

"How did delaying telling me delay you leaving? You could have told me, and we could have figured it out together."

Ben shook his head. "I'm not talking about me leaving. Yes, me leaving is inevitable, but I'm talking about our relationship. I'm talking about how unrealistic long-distance relationships are."

Liza had been angry with Ben for keeping this from her, but suddenly, all of her emotions drained away. It felt like someone had pulled a plug and all of her frustration and anger and fear washed away, leaving behind only disbelief.

She felt numb.

"You're breaking up with me?"

Ben couldn't even answer. He looked down at the ground, avoiding her eyes, and Liza was actually grateful for it. She didn't want him to see that she was crying.

"You don't even want to try?" she asked.

"I don't see the point. I'm going to be on the other side of the world, and I don't know where I'll go next. Or if I'll make it out."

"Don't say that." Liza couldn't even let herself think that was a possibility.

"See?" Ben stepped forward and grabbed Liza's hand. She wanted to pull away, but despite everything, the warmth of his fingers around hers was comforting. "I don't want to put you through this. I don't want to leave you at home while you worry about me, wondering where I am and if I'm okay. It's not fair to you."

"None of this is fair," Liza croaked. "None of this is okay."

Ben squeezed her hand once and then backed away, clearing his throat. "It will be better for you—for both of us—if you just move on. Move on, and I'll do the same."

Before Liza could even respond, Ben turned around and left. It was the last time Liza would see him for three decades.

18

Ben's mouth fell open and his arm dropped to his side. For a second, Liza thought he might be angry. It was his sister's wedding after all. Maybe he was mad at her for ruining the evening by bringing up their past. Maybe she shouldn't have. Maybe she should have—

Suddenly, he looked around the room, grabbed Liza's hand, and pulled them both towards the double doors at the back of the barn that opened out onto a patio.

It was cold outside, so guests sitting at tables nearby yelped when Ben opened the door, but he didn't seem to notice.

He closed the door behind them and looked around the patio to make sure they were alone. Then, he turned to Liza, tipped his head to the side with a sad smile, and sighed.

"I've been wondering when you'd want to talk about this."

Liza felt self-conscious suddenly. "I'm sorry. Maybe your sister's wedding isn't the right time to—"

"No, I'm glad," he said, wrapping his warm fingers around her chilled hands. "I'm relieved. I've wanted to talk to you about everything, but I didn't want to force anything on you. You made it clear early on that you didn't want to talk to me, period, so I didn't want to push my luck."

"I shouldn't have said that," Liza started.

"Yes, you should have." Ben dipped his chin and looked at her under heavy brows. "I deserved it, Liza. I deserved worse. You've been incredibly kind to me considering what I did. How I left."

"You're hard to resist." The admission was another stone loosened from the wall around her heart, but Liza couldn't keep it in. It was the truth. Whatever it was about Ben that drew her in, it was effective. She couldn't force herself to stay away from him, regardless of how afraid she was he'd hurt her again.

He smiled and took another deep breath. "So are you, Liza Hall. I've always been drawn to you."

"Then why did you leave?" Liza asked again. Inside, the question had been spur of the moment, reckless. But now, she wanted to know. She was ready to know.

"At the time, I didn't even understand why I left." He must have seen the confusion that crossed her face because he stepped closer to her, folding her hands in his and pressing them to his chest. "I know it would make us both feel better if I had some grand, noble reason, but I want to be honest with you. I was young—we both were—and I didn't know how to deal with what the two of us were doing."

"Dating?"

"Being in love," Ben whispered. "I didn't know how to be in love with you and complete my goals. I wasn't ready for how much loving you would change everything for me. When we started talking in the bar and hanging out together, I didn't know what I was getting into. Maybe if I had, I would've stayed away from you. But I'm glad I didn't know. Because I'm grateful every day for the year we spent together."

Liza didn't know how she should feel. "Are you saying you couldn't stay with me because you loved me too much?"

He chuckled and shook his head. "It sounds ridiculous, but kind of? I was too immature for what we were doing, but now..."

"Now?" Liza's heart was fluttering in her chest. She did her best to swallow down her nerves, but she could feel her hands trembling.

"I can't help but feel like this is all fate, Liza."

Liza shivered, and Ben slipped out of his jacket and laid it over her shoulders. Then, he pulled her close, wrapping his hands around her waist.

"I don't want to rush you," he continued. "And I don't want to freak you out. It's not like I've been pining for you for thirty years, waiting for the day when our paths would cross."

"You weren't stalking me?" Liza asked, sliding her arms around his neck.

"No, I'm afraid not." He smiled. "Are you disappointed?"

"No. I was just asking to see if I needed to scream for help or file a restraining order."

"I don't think that's necessary."

"Okay, great. Sorry to interrupt. Continue."

He tipped his head back and laughed before smiling down at her. "I didn't just sit and wait for you. As you know, I had a daughter. I had a life. I traveled and lived. But I never forgot you, Liza. Deep down, I always hoped I'd run into you again. If only to see you in person, apologize, and mend a part of my past I've always felt was unfinished."

Liza related to that feeling. As much as she tried to push Ben out of her conscious thoughts, she always felt like the ending to their story was unsatisfactory. She always thought there should be more.

"And then I found you here, in Willow Beach of all places, and it feels like life has finally brought us back together. It feels like the right time. We're both single, and I know now that the only thing I want to accomplish in my life is to be happy, and I am happy when I'm with you. It feels like this could work. Doesn't it?" His mouth twisted nervously to the side.

"It does." The words slipped out before Liza could truly consider them, but she knew they were true.

If she didn't think she and Ben had a chance, she wouldn't be having this conversation with him. There would be no point. But she'd asked him to explain his actions to her because she hoped she could forgive him and move forward. She hoped she could trust him again, and now, finally, she felt like she could.

"It feels like it could work," she said, her eyes glossing over with happy tears. "I want it to work."

Ben grinned and brought a hand to her cheek, smoothing his thumb over her cheekbone. "I want it to work, too, Liza. I'm ready for this. For you."

Liza curled her fingers in the hair at the nape of his neck. "Took you long enough."

Without warning, Ben bent down and pressed his lips to Liza's.

The kiss wasn't earth-shattering and knee-quaking. It was gentle. It spoke to their history and to their still-tender hearts. Ben wasn't trying to sweep Liza off her feet and wow her with a whirlwind romance. They didn't want an explosion; they wanted an eternal flame. This was the spark that would light it.

Hot and heavy or not, Liza felt Ben's kiss in every part of her.

She curled her fingers around his neck as he gripped her hips and pulled her close, and she squeezed her eyes closed, absorbing every second of the embrace.

It had been a long time since she'd been kissed like this. Not only because she'd been divorced for three years, but because Liza and Cliff never kissed like this.

"You two are like chickens," Liza's mom had said to her one year at Thanksgiving. "Pecking at one another out of habit."

Liza had assured her mom she and Cliff did enough kissing in their alone time, but it was a lie. She and Cliff rarely kissed. Just a quick hello, a quick goodbye, a quick good night. It was routine and emotionless. Nothing like kissing Ben.

Ben smoothed his hands up Liza's back and beneath the jacket he'd thrown over her shoulders. He gripped her shoulder blades and seemed to inhale as the kiss ended, like he was breathing in as much of her as was possible.

They pressed their foreheads together and smiled, and they could have been twenty-somethings again. Liza felt young and light and carefree.

She felt like she was in love.

"No way," Ben whispered.

Liza pulled away, thinking something was wrong, and then she followed Ben's gaze upward to the sky. And the snow.

"It's snowing," she said, mostly to herself.

"I can't believe it. It's snowing. Again."

Again. Just like it had been the first time they'd kissed.

"Can you believe this?" Ben asked, wrapping his arm around her waist and pulling her against his side as he watching the fat flakes fall.

Liza nestled against his side and shook her head, smiling so hard she thought her cheeks would start to cramp. "No," she said. "I can't believe any of it."

19

When someone knocked on the cottage's front door a few days after the wedding, Liza called from the kitchen for Ben to come on inside.

"Door's open!"

She was surprised he was knocking at all, honestly. He'd been coming over regularly enough that Liza had started leaving the door unlocked for him.

When I have my own place, I'll make him a key, she thought.

"Wow, Aunt Liza! This town must be safe if you're just going to let people waltz right into your house."

At the sound of her niece's voice, Liza dropped her cookie cutter on the counter and spun around. "Angela?"

Angela appeared in the kitchen doorway and waved. She had on a pair of overalls with an oversized knit sweater underneath. Her hair was pulled back in a high bun with a colorful scarf wrapped around the base. She was boho-chic and lovely, and a genuine sight for sore eyes.

"Why do you seem surprised to see me?" Angela asked. "You knew I was coming."

Yes, Liza had known, but she'd forgotten. Entirely.

The three days after Stacy's wedding had been a whirlwind. Not only because Liza had to package all of the leftover food up for Stacy and Ben's parents to take home and pick up all of her stuff from Georgia's kitchen at the inn, but also because she and Ben had spent every spare second together discussing their plans for the future.

Plans that involved Liza staying in Willow Beach.

The decision wasn't entirely based on Ben. After all, he didn't even live in Willow Beach. He was only visiting for his sister's wedding.

But Liza liked the town. She liked the friends she met, and even if she didn't end up staying forever, she didn't see why she couldn't make her time there slightly more open-ended.

She was thinking about ending her lease on the kitchen space she rented in Boston and moving her headquarters to Willow Beach. Or, she could keep the space in Boston and hire a few more cooks to work out of it while Liza herself was stationed in Willow Beach. It was only a couple of hours to Boston, anyway, so Liza could make the drive as often as she needed to in order to meet with clients.

"I work entirely online," Ben had said in encouragement of the plan. "You can do consultations over video chat or the phone and meet up to taste-test food. It's not a problem."

That had sounded crazy at first, but the more she thought about it, the more she saw a way it could really all work.

"Of course, I knew you were coming," Liza said to Angela. "I just didn't think you'd be here so early."

Angela dropped her purse, keys, and phone on the counter with Liza's stuff. "Am I interrupting anything?"

Liza glanced at the clock above the stove and yelped. "Actually, you're a lifesaver. I have an appointment scheduled, and I almost missed it. I got a little lost in rolling out this cookie dough."

"Gingerbread cookies," Angela sighed, smelling the air. Then, she shook her head as if clearing her thoughts and frowned. "What appointment? We were supposed to do coffee at eleven. And I only scheduled you the one wedding. Aunt Liza! Did you schedule more work? This is supposed to be a vacation."

"I didn't schedule more work, I swear." Liza untied her apron and hung it on the hook next to the fridge. "And we can still get coffee afterward. This is an appointment about a rental property, actually."

As Liza darted around, slipping on her shoes and grabbing her coat, Angela followed, peppering her with questions. "What rental property? An apartment? In Willow Beach? Are you moving? Are you retiring from catering? Do I need to find a new job?"

Finally, Liza grabbed Angela by the shoulders and looked her in the eyes. "Come with me, and I'll explain everything in the car."

~

Liza explained her plan for running the catering company from Willow Beach to Angela with no small amount of nerves. As much as the business belonged to Liza, it belonged to Angela, too. They were in this together, and Liza didn't know what she would do if Angela didn't agree with her decision.

"So, you really like it here, then?" Angela asked. "Beach life is your thing?"

Liza laughed and turned onto Main Street. "Apparently. I love the sound of the ocean and the people are all so friendly. I never thought I'd want to leave the city, but these last few weeks have changed my mind."

Angela turned to Liza, eyes narrowed. "Are you sure *someone* hasn't changed your mind too? Didn't you have a date not too long ago?"

"I wouldn't make a decision like this only because of a man."

"I didn't say *only* because of a man," Angela countered. "But maybe a man played a small part? Wasn't his name Ben?"

Liza couldn't help but smile at the mention of his name, and Angela snapped her fingers and pointed. "Aha. There it is. The truth!"

Liza pursed her lips and rolled her eyes. "Just tell me what you think. Do you think it makes sense for me to stay here for a while? It's not like I have a place to live in Boston, anyway."

"Aunt Liza, I want you to do whatever makes you happy. I'm convinced that you can taste your happiness in your food. If you are happy, your food is better, and better food is good for business."

"Are you sure?"

"Positive," Angela said with a confident nod.

Liza pulled into a parking space on the right side of Main Street in front of an empty storefront. "That's good, because I'm here to look at a business space."

Angela squealed, and the two women walked into the appointment arm in arm.

~

"What do you think? Do either of you have any questions?" Ramon, the landlord, was an intimidating man at well over six feet tall, but he was as friendly as anyone Liza had ever met. Liza would be happy to have him as her landlord.

"It's perfect," Angela said, pressing her hands to her heard. "The exposed brick, the pressed-tin ceilings, the natural daylight. It's a dream."

"I like it fine," Liza said, trying to counter Angela's enthusiasm.

"I *love* it. My only question: where do we sign?"

Liza laughed. "Okay, hold on. We still need to think about this. It's a great space, but I don't want to rush into anything."

"That's smart, Ms. Hall," Ramon said. "I obviously want to get a great business in this space as soon as possible, but the demand for retail spaces in Willow Beach isn't so high that you need to make any commitments right this very second. You have time to think about it."

That was great because Liza really did need time to think.

She had come to Willow Beach to get out of her rut and look towards her future, but now that she was looking at staying in Willow Beach, she couldn't help but wonder if she wasn't just staying because it was easy. Because she'd already made friends and was comfortable here.

Was it similar to the way she'd agreed to marry Cliff, assuming she'd fall in love with him eventually?

She told herself it was different. Liza didn't need to fall in love with Willow Beach; she already loved it. And it certainly didn't feel like settling.

Still, she worried she was falling back into old habits.

Liza and Angela walked the two blocks down to The Roast for coffee, and when Liza walked through the door, her eyes landed on Ben standing at the counter.

Speaking of old habits.

He turned around and beamed, almost as if he'd been expecting her. "Liza. Fancy running into you here."

Angela gasped and then whispered, "Is that Ben? Is that him?"

Liza ignored her and focused instead on the almond croissant in Ben's hand. "Ben Boyd, how on earth did you get an almond croissant midmorning? They are usually sold out before nine."

"It is him," Angela sighed, doing very little to keep her voice down. "He's so handsome."

Ben shrugged slyly and handed Liza the croissant. "I came in and bought it this morning. Vivienne was kind enough to hold it for me."

Never one to turn down sugary carbs, Liza accepted the croissant. As she grabbed it, Ben pulled her close and gave her a quick yet passionate kiss on the mouth. Once they broke apart, Liza took a big bite of the croissant to hide how flushed she was. "How did you know I'd be here today? Did I mention it to you?"

Before Ben could answer, Angela stepped forward, hand extended. "I'm Liza's niece and business partner, Angela."

"I've heard a lot about you," Ben said, tipping his head.

"All good things, I hope?" Angela eyed Liza suspiciously, and Liza nudged her ornery niece towards a table in the corner.

Angela and Ben hit it off great. Liza hadn't realized how much Angela and Ben were alike, but now that they were together at the table, both lovingly teasing Liza and exuding a pure joy for life, Liza couldn't unsee it.

Suddenly, it made perfect sense why Liza had fallen for Ben twice and why she and Angela got along so well. The things that made Ben a great boyfriend were the same things that made Angela a good partner.

"So, you're the man who is stealing my aunt away from the big city?" Angela shook her head and sipped on her cappuccino. "I suppose I can understand why. If any man interested in me was this handsome, I'd also betray my family."

"I'm not betraying my family! You said it sounded like a good idea!"

"It is!" Angela smiled at them both. "I think it's great."

Liza's phone buzzed in her pocket, but she ignored it. It was probably about work or Dora sending her yet another picture of her wearing a tank top in December with the message: *"This could be you."* Either way, Liza wanted to give all of her attention to the two people sitting in front of her.

"I'm not sure how long I'll even stay, so renting the kitchen space feels a little premature."

"But where would you work from?" Angela asked. "You need a proper kitchen."

"I was going to cater Stacy's wedding from the cottage's kitchen just fine."

"And then the oven broke," Ben reminded her.

Liza elbowed him as her phone vibrated again. "Whose side are you on?"

"Your side. Or whichever side means you and I end up in the same place," he said, holding his hands up in surrender.

Angela nodded approvingly. "Smart man."

"Well, I emailed Mrs. Albertson about house-sitting the cottage for the entire length of her trip, but she hasn't messaged back. If she agrees, that gives me a place to live for five months."

"What about Ben?" Angela asked. "You're not from Willow Beach, right?"

"No, but I freelance. I can live anywhere with an internet connection."

"Like the cottage!"

Liza's eyes widened in warning, but her niece was too caught up in the moment to notice.

"You two could totally live in the cottage together. It's free, big enough for the two of you, and it's basically a vacation in a bottle. Right on the beach, within walking distance of the entire Main Street shopping and restaurant district. This place is so romantic."

"That is certainly something Ben and I will discuss later. Alone. When you are not here," Liza said, placing special emphasis on the last two sentences.

Angela backed down, but Liza heard her mutter "just saying" into her coffee mug.

"I can rent a place downtown," Ben added, trying to break the tension. "Or stay at the inn for a while longer. It's pricier than a rental, but I have some good savings."

"Financially responsible, too." Angela wagged her brows at Liza, and Liza was beginning to have regrets about introducing her niece to her beau.

When a text message alert buzzed for the third time, Liza decided a text from Dora would be a welcome distraction, so she finally pulled out her phone.

Immediately, she realized the phone wasn't hers. It was Angela's. Liza must have grabbed it off the counter by mistake in her rush to get out the door.

She was about to hand it back when the phone buzzed a fourth time and she saw an unsettlingly familiar name flash on the screen: **Heather Boyd.**

Just a couple of weeks earlier, Angela had acted like she had no idea who Heather was, and now she had Ben's daughter's number in her phone? That didn't make sense.

Liza knew she should just ask Angela about it, but curiosity got the best of her, and she swiped up on the screen. She'd been telling Angela for years to set a passcode on her phone—it was one of the few subjects where Liza was more tech savvy—but she never had, and suddenly, Liza was grateful.

A string of messages appeared.

Are you at the coffee shop yet? My dad should be there already.

He's going to leave if you don't hurry.

Are you getting these? Is the plan working?

ARE THEY IN LOVE YET?!

Liza read the messages once and then again, trying to think of any explanation other than the one already in her head. She didn't want to think Angela and Ben would lie to her, but wasn't this proof they had?

Ben had spoken to Liza about fate...destiny. But this wasn't destiny.

Are they in love yet?

Someone along the way had manipulated fate. Suddenly, Liza felt ridiculously naïve.

20

Whether Ben was scared away by Angela's meddling or he sensed the tension in the air and decided it was safest to leave, Liza didn't know, but she didn't stop him when he said he should let them enjoy coffee on their own.

Liza wanted to speak with Angela more than anyone.

As soon as Ben walked out of the front door, the bell jangling to announce his departure, Liza turned to her niece.

"He's so handsome," Angela said. "Tall and broad-shouldered and his eyes. Oh, Aunt Liza, his eyes. He's a dreamboat! I can't believe you didn't send me pictures!"

Liza slid Angela her phone, the screen opened to Heather's string of unanswered messages. "I didn't need to. I'm sure Heather already showed you one, right?"

Angela blinked as the reality of the situation washed over her. Her eyes skimmed over Heather's messages and then flicked back to Liza's face. Her cheeks were pale.

"Aunt Liza, I can explain."

"Was this all a game to you?" Liza asked, struggling to keep her voice from shaking. "Did you think your aunt's life was so miserable that you needed to treat her like she was on a game show? Did the two of you have fun laughing at me?"

"No! That isn't at all what happened. Let me explain."

"How much did Ben know?" Liza asked, but as soon as the question was out of her mouth, she shook her head. "No. I'll ask him myself. I want him to explain his part in all of this to my face, but I wanted to talk to you first. Because I trusted you."

Angela's face fell. "Trusted? Past tense? You don't trust me anymore?"

"How can I, Angela? You've been lying to me. I asked you if you knew Heather, and you acted like you didn't."

"Okay, yes. I lied about that, but—"

"And why is Ben in Willow Beach?"

Angela bit her lower lip. "For his sister's wedding."

Liza raised one brow in an unspoken threat. "Why did you choose Willow Beach as the place where I should come to relax? Why did you book me as the caterer for Stacy's wedding?"

"Because you're a talented caterer, and I knew you'd kill it."

"Angela!" Liza yelled, slapping the table and drawing the attention of Vivienne behind the counter. She quickly realized something serious was going on and turned away, pretending to go back to her work, though Liza was sure she was eavesdropping. Liza couldn't blame her. If this wasn't happening to her, she would be listening in, too.

"I'm sorry." Angela folded her hands around her half-empty coffee mug and sighed. "Heather found your name in a letter or something when she was in her dad's office. She looked you up online, saw a picture of me in your photos, and she reached out. We pieced together a bit of your history from everywhere we could, and it seemed like a really romantic story. Heather wanted her dad to be happy, and I wanted you to be happy, and we thought maybe we could solve both problems at the same time. Her aunt was getting married, my aunt is a caterer—it seemed like fate was on our side."

"This isn't fate," Liza grumbled. "It's manipulation."

"You agreed to come to Willow Beach and do the wedding."

"Under false pretenses, Angela. If I'd known Ben was going to be here, I would have refused to come."

Angela clenched her fists and went wide-eyed. "Don't you see? That's why I didn't tell you. You *did* come to Willow Beach, you *did* reconnect with him, and now the two of you are happy. I didn't want your stubbornness to get in the way."

"My stubbornness?" Liza asked, standing up so quickly her chair nearly tipped over. "This isn't about my stubbornness; it's about my pride. My self-respect. I'm capable of finding my own partners and satisfying my own romantic needs. I don't need to be tricked into it."

"But it wasn't a trick!" Angela exclaimed. "The only thing we did is make sure the two of you were in the same place at the same time. You did the rest."

Liza pointed to Angela's phone. "It sounds like maybe today's meeting was arranged?"

Angela chewed on the corner of her lip nervously, and Liza shook her head. "How am I supposed to trust you if you keep lying to me? How am I supposed to trust anything anyone has said to me?"

"You can trust Ben!"

Liza snorted. "Oh, can I?"

"Yes. He knew you were going to be the caterer, but that's all."

Liza wanted to believe Angela. She wanted to believe that Ben was as innocent a bystander in all of this as she was, but it became harder and harder to believe that.

Just within the last ten minutes, she'd point-blank asked him whose side he was on.

Your side. Or whichever side means you and I end up in the same place.

There it was. He'd as good as admitted it...right? He'd been willing to set this whole romance up while Liza was completely in the dark. He'd waxed on about fate and destiny and the universe, all the while knowing that their reunion had been arranged. All the while knowing what his end goal was.

And if Ben knew all along that he wanted to try and get Liza back—even before he knew her as a fifty-four-year-old rather than the twenty-something she'd been when they met—wouldn't that sway the results? It's the same reason researchers often don't tell research subjects the nature of the study. They don't want to corrupt the results.

Well, the results of this experiment had been corrupted from the jump.

Ben had gone into this hoping to win, hoping to gain Liza's trust and her love, and he'd succeeded. Swimmingly.

Unfortunately, Liza no longer knew what was real and what was simply his attempt to complete his objective.

Liza couldn't trust anyone, and after this experience, she didn't know if she ever would again.

"Let me fix it," Angela said desperately, tears in her eyes. "I screwed up, but you don't have to blow everything up. Let me talk to Ben and explain things to him, and then he can explain things to you and... just, please, let me fix it."

Liza shook her head. "There's no fixing this."

~

Liza turned off her phone, locked her front door, and hid away in the bedroom of the cottage she'd come to call home, however temporarily.

For a minute, she'd thought she had it all figured out, but once again, the rug had been ripped out from underneath her. But you can't fall down if you don't stand up.

So, Liza stayed in bed the rest of the day and the rest of the night.

When someone knocked on the front door, she pulled the blanket over her head and went to sleep.

She didn't want to talk to anyone.

21

Liza stayed inside the next day, too.

She didn't know if Angela had gone back to Boston or if Ben was trying to call her. For all she knew, he'd left Willow Beach. Maybe now that the plot had been revealed, he wouldn't be interested in her anymore. Maybe her knowing about the plan would ruin his good time.

It didn't seem fair to judge him so harshly based on what little information she had, but then again, Liza wasn't in the mood to be fair to anyone.

She'd put herself out there. After the way he'd hurt her in the past, Liza had pushed away all of her doubts and insecurities and trusted him, and now she was paying the price.

As a form of comfort or self-punishment—Liza couldn't be sure—she ordered pizza the night before, ate cold pizza for breakfast, and then reheated the last of the pizza for lunch. By dinner, she felt bloated and miserable, but she was still thinking about ordering another pizza.

Maybe a veggie pizza, she thought. As though that would make much of a difference.

Instead, she finally got out of bed, put on some real clothes—if leggings and a long sweater can be called "real clothes"—and went into the kitchen. She didn't make anything fancy, but she whipped together a quick vegetable soup and a grilled cheese. It made her feel a bit more human, which was a step up.

On her way back to the bedroom, Liza caught a glimpse of her reflection in a mirror in the hallway, and it was bleak. Shocking, really.

Her face was oily from not washing off her makeup the night before, her hair was sticking up in eighteen different directions, and she looked years older. She knew that wasn't possible, but the lines around her mouth seemed more pronounced, and there were bags under her eyes.

It was pathetic.

She was pathetic.

Yes, she'd been betrayed for the second time by the man she loved—and love him she did, despite her unwillingness to admit it—and now she had no idea what she wanted to do with her life.

Except, maybe she that wasn't quite true.

Even if Ben wasn't in the picture anymore, didn't Liza still love Willow Beach? Did she still want to be close to the beach and attend book club meetings with Georgia and Stella and the rest of the women?

Yes to both. Liza didn't need to throw away her entire plan because of one act of betrayal.

The realization provided a slight boost to her morale, and Liza marched into the bathroom and took a shower. She lathered and rinsed her hair twice, scrubbed her face free of makeup, and brushed her teeth for the first time all day. By the time she was finished, she felt marginally better. Still not good enough to rejoin society, but good enough to go for a walk.

She towel-dried her hair and then tucked the damp locks up into a hat, shoved her socked feet into a pair of boots, and pulled on her long puffy coat. Then she set off down to the beach.

Thanksgiving was only a few weeks away, and the wind off the ocean was icy. It seemed to slice through Liza's clothes, but she didn't hate the sensation. In fact, she liked the harshness of it. The weather matched her mood, and Liza plopped right down in the sand, close enough that she was in danger of getting wet from the tide.

She would stay in Willow Beach.

The decision came to her easily. It's what she wanted. Part of the sadness she'd felt over the last twenty-four hours was at this perfect little town being stolen away from her, but it didn't need to be. The only thing that had really been stolen from her was the future she'd imagined with Ben.

As soon as Ben had reappeared in her life, Liza worried she was regressing. She'd promised herself Willow Beach would be a fresh start, but here she was thirty years later dealing with the same devastation she'd dealt with at twenty-four.

Liza considered herself to be a rational, logical person, yet she couldn't seem to be rational or logical when it came to Ben. For reasons Liza would never understand, he had a direct line to her heart, and she couldn't resist.

That was what made the betrayal so much worse.

Liza thought, naively, that the way she was naturally drawn to Ben must be fate. Maybe it was the universe's way of whispering to her, *This one. He's the one. Love him.*

Now, Liza likened it to the decision-making skills a drunk person has. Ben intoxicated Liza, and she couldn't think clearly. That wasn't a good thing. It was a dangerous thing.

Still, she couldn't seem to convince herself of that. Even knowing everything she knew about Angela and Heather's plans, Liza wanted to believe Ben was innocent. She wanted to forgive him. She wanted to be with him.

She didn't realize she was crying until her face grew painfully cold. The wind off the water was drying her tears to her cheeks, and she swiped at them with gloved hands and then buried her face in the circle of her arms.

Liza didn't know how long she stayed that way, but when she lifted her head, she wasn't alone.

Liza screamed and rolled sideways in surprise, and Stella slapped her hands over her mouth. "Liza, I'm so sorry!"

A scream died in her throat, and Liza fell back in the sand as her heartbeat returned to normal pace. "You scared the tar out of me, Stella! When did you get here?"

"Five minutes ago," she said, smiling guiltily. "I didn't want to disturb you."

"You should have disturbed me. If you had, maybe I wouldn't have been so scared when I looked up." Liza shook her head and pressed a hand to her chest. "I almost had a heart attack."

"I'm sorry." Stella chuckled a bit and clapped a hand on Liza's back. "I didn't come to scare you. I actually came to check on you."

Liza bit her lip, unsure how much to divulge. What did Stella know? Did everyone in Willow Beach know what had happened? Was this plan even more elaborate than Liza had thought?

"Sam saw you leaving The Roast yesterday, and he said you looked upset. I came by the house last night and this morning, but you didn't answer. Finally, I thought I'd check the beach, and here we are."

"You came to check on me?" Liza didn't know why she was surprised, but she was.

"Of course! That's what friends are for."

Liza liked Stella and all the women from the book club, but she kind of assumed it was a one-way street. At least for right now. They were all friends, and had been for a while, whereas Liza was a newcomer, and a temporary one, at that.

"That's really nice of you."

"It's lucky I found you, actually," Stella said. "I was getting pretty close to asking the sheriff to come do a wellness check."

"I was...off the grid for a while," Liza explained.

"Yeah, I asked Ben if he'd heard from you, but he seemed a little upset too. I thought maybe he might have something to do with why you disappeared."

Liza nodded, her lower lip trembling. Then, without warning, she began to cry.

Really, truly cry.

Between sobs, the story came out. Liza told Stella about her past with Ben, why she'd come to Willow Beach, and about her niece's role in the deception. She told Stella how duped she felt, how manipulated and embarrassed. She told her about the nature of her marriage with Cliff, about the last three years she'd spent in her small apartment in Boston, and about how much she loved Willow Beach and had started imagining a future for herself there.

Liza told Stella more than she'd ever planned or hoped, and when she was done, she felt...relieved. Lighter, somehow.

She studied Stella, watching for signs that she'd unloaded far too much information on the woman. Instead, however, Liza saw pure empathy written in every line of Stella's face.

"Oh, Liza," Stella said, wrapping her arm around Liza and pulling her close. "I'm so sorry."

"It's okay. It's what I get for putting myself out there."

"No!" Stella barked, the forcefulness of it surprising Liza. "No, that is not 'what you get.' Nobody deserves to be hurt for making themselves vulnerable. Plus—and I don't want to offend you, so take this as it is intended—have you considered that Ben didn't know about any of this?"

"I'm not offended. I have considered that, but I'm not sure if it matters. At the end of the day, he and I both thought our reunion was fate, but now it seems it was all arranged."

Stella bit her lower lip. "So?"

"So?" Liza repeated. "So, that means our love isn't destiny."

"Who says? Maybe it was destiny for your meddling niece to get involved in your love life and get you and Ben in the same town again."

Liza hadn't thought of it that way, but she didn't know if that mattered. "I feel like an idiot. I'm not sure I can look at him the same way without feeling embarrassed. I'm so pathetic my niece had to interfere in my love life."

"Or," Stella said, lifting a finger. "You're so loved that your niece wanted to help you find an amazing guy."

"You should work in politics. You're very good at spinning this story from negative to positive."

Stella shrugged. "It's a gift."

Liza was grateful for Stella's perspective, and it had made her feel slightly better, but she wasn't ready to stop wallowing just yet.

"I totally get the need to wallow, believe me, but I think you should push pause on wallowing at least for tonight and come with me to an art show."

For the first time, Liza took in Stella's appearance, and realized she was wearing a black dress with tights and booties, and her hair was curled and pinned back with a silver clip.

"Wow. You look amazing."

Stella beamed. "Thank you. As the featured artist, I figured it was only appropriate that I look the part."

Liza's eyes widened. "You're the featured artist? As in, the art show is all of your work?"

"It sounds fancy, but it's really not that big of the deal. I just finished a collection of pieces themed around the intersection of light and dark, and I wanted to hold a small showing for family and friends and potential customers. There won't be too many people there, but there will be food and wine. I think it will be fun."

Liza had to admit, it did sound nice. However...

She looked down at her own appearance and frowned. "I'm a mess."

"That is true," Stella said, laughing when Liza wrinkled her nose at her. "But you have plenty of time to fix it. Run home, get dressed, and meet me at the gallery downtown."

Liza knew right away which gallery Stella was talking about. It was only a few spaces down from the rental space Liza had looked at with Angela yesterday.

Yesterday. Was that really how little time had passed since everything in Liza's life had imploded? It seemed hard to believe. It felt like she'd been in bed for at least a week. Which was probably the main reason why it was time that Liza got out of bed and rejoined the living.

"Sure, okay. I'll come."

Stella clapped and threw her arms around Liza. "I'm so glad. I really wanted you to be there."

Liza hugged her back. "And I really want to be there."

It was true. Liza did want to be there.

At the art gallery.

And in Willow Beach.

She wanted to live here, and nothing would stop her.

22

Liza lightly curled her hair, swiped some mascara on her lashes and blush across her cheeks, and pulled on the sweater dress she'd worn on her date with Ben. For a second, her hand hesitated over the dress, wondering if she should wear it or if it would bring up bad memories. Or, really, if it would bring up good memories, which would make her feel bad.

In the end, though, Liza decided it was high time to let go of the past.

She wasn't going to keep herself from enjoying her favorite things—like her beautiful olive- green sweater dress that fit her like a glove—because she was afraid of being hurt or upset. It was time to stop running and, as Stella had suggested that day on the beach several weeks ago, face the pain from her past and work through it.

It was also time to decide on a path for her future.

Before she left, Liza pulled out her phone and called Ramon, the landlord for the rental space on Main.

"Hey, Ramon, it's Liza Hall from the showing yesterday. I'm calling about renting the space. I love it, and I'd like to set up a lease."

"Oh, Liza, hey." Ramon sounded off, not nearly as friendly as he had the day before. "I'm so sorry, but the space is actually no longer available."

"Oh..." He'd told her she had plenty of time. Liza assumed that meant more than twenty-four hours. She wanted to ask why it wasn't available. Had someone else rented it? Was he no longer trying to lease it? Had it been destroyed in a fire?

However, Ramon didn't seem like he wanted to give out any details, so Liza didn't feel it was her place to ask. She thanked him for his time and hung up.

"It's fine," she said out loud to herself, lifting her chin and taking a deep breath. "I can still have a good night."

She'd been unsure about the kitchen space, anyway. Yes, it was beautiful and well-lit and the perfect place to host tastings with clients, but she could figure something else out. This didn't mean her dream of living in Willow Beach was dead. It just meant it was different now.

Liza drove down Main Street and parked in the space in front of the gallery. She could see people milling around inside—Georgia, Sam, Alma and Gwen, Vivienne and her husband—and the space looked amazing. Even from outside, Liza could see some of the canvases hanging on the walls with lights positioned above them, illuminating Stella's incredible talent.

Just as she was about to walk through the gallery doors, though, the artist herself burst through them and grabbed her arm.

"Can you help me?" Stella asked, seeming slightly frantic.

"Of course. What's going on?"

Stella pulled Liza down the sidewalk wordlessly.

"Is everything okay?" Liza asked. "Is something wrong with your show? It looked like it was going well from what I could say."

"The show is fine. There's just something else I need your help with."

Stella seemed flustered. Her cheeks were red and flushed, and she couldn't look Liza in the eye.

Liza followed her for a few more steps before she pulled on Stella's arm, forcing the woman to face her. "What is going on?"

"You'll find out when we get there."

"No." Liza crossed her arms and stared at Stella. "I'm going to find out right now. Where are you taking me?"

For the first time, Stella looked in Liza's eyes. She seemed nervous, but sincere. "Liza, do you trust me?"

Trust.

That had become a tough word for Liza recently.

She wasn't sure she really trusted anyone. She couldn't trust Angela —at least not as much as she'd thought.

She couldn't trust Ben.

She couldn't even trust Ramon. Because of him, she'd lost out on the kitchen space, which was actually only one more storefront ahead of where she was currently standing.

Still, Liza *wanted* to trust Stella, and she supposed that meant more than anything else.

"Yes," she said. "I trust you."

Stella gave her a small smile. "Okay. Then please come with me, and try not to be mad. Okay?"

Well, that was not exactly a comforting sentence, but Liza did her best to shove down her uncertainty. Stella was her friend, and if Liza was ever going to trust anyone again, she had to start somewhere. Why not here?

Stella pulled Liza down the street and stopped directly in front of the kitchen space she'd looked at the day before. Despite what Ramon had said on the phone, the "for lease" sign was still hanging in the paper-covered windows.

"What are we doing here?"

"You said you want to stay in Willow Beach, right?" Stella asked.

Liza frowned. "This space isn't available anymore."

Stella waved a hand to dismiss Liza's words. "That isn't what I asked. You want to stay here, right?"

"Yes," Liza said. "I do."

"And you trust me, right?"

Liza took a deep breath and nodded. "Yes, I trust you."

"Okay, then trust me when I say that we only had your best interests at heart, okay?"

"We?"

Stella ignored that question, pulled open the front door of the vacant space, and pushed Liza inside. Instead of coming in with her, Stella pulled the door closed, leaving Liza inside alone. The room was too dark to make out anything except a few dark smudges, but suddenly, an overhead light flicked on.

Liza blinked against the sudden brightness, and then heard a familiar, deep laugh. "Sorry about that."

She froze, staring straight ahead as her vision cleared and Benjamin Boyd came into view.

He was standing in the middle of the room, next to a small camping stove. The lid was on it, but smoke was coming out of the top, and Liza could see a small flame sputtering through the grate.

"What's going on?" Her voice sounded cold, and Ben flinched.

He stepped forward and then stopped when he noticed her retreat back a step. "We need to talk."

"I don't want to talk." It was an echo of what she'd told him a few weeks ago. "That's why I turned my phone off."

"I know," he said. "I want to respect your wishes, but I also can't stand the idea that you think I betrayed you."

Liza crossed her arms, an old defense mechanism. "But didn't you?"

"No," he said, sounding desperate. "Liza, no, I didn't. I wouldn't."

"I saw the text messages on Angela's phone. She and Heather had a plan to get us together. You're telling me you didn't know about it? You didn't know I was going to be here in Willow Beach."

He snapped and pointed at her. "Okay, yes. I did know you were going to be the caterer to the wedding, but I found out a day before I arrived in Willow Beach. I didn't schedule for you to be the caterer or decide to stay in Willow Beach and help with wedding stuff because of that. I agreed to stay in Willow Beach to help Stacy, and *then* I learned you'd be the caterer. It was a very happy coincidence."

Liza wanted to believe him desperately, but she wasn't sure.

"The night my water pipe burst, you came to help me."

"I was being honest about that. I told you I saw you in the parking lot and then came down to help, but I didn't plan for your pipe to burst or anything. Again, just another happy coincidence."

Liza frowned. "What about the coffee shop yesterday? It seemed like Heather told you Angela and I would be there."

He shook his head. "No, she didn't. I told Heather about you as soon as we reconnected. She and I talk about everything, and she encouraged me to go after you. I told you she loves croissants, so of course, she suggested I go to The Roast to buy you a croissant and take it to the cottage as a surprise. I was just as surprised as you were when you and Angela walked into the coffee shop together."

Liza was still hesitant. "Okay, that makes sense. Maybe I was a little too quick to blame you given our history."

"I know, and I understand that. But I swear, I wouldn't ever purposefully do anything to hurt you," Ben said. "As eager as I was to come to Willow Beach and see you again, I wouldn't have gone behind your back to orchestrate all of this. I want our relationship to be real."

"That's just it," Liza said. "This isn't real. It wasn't orchestrated by you, but it was still orchestrated."

He lifted a shoulder in a shrug, his mouth twisted to the side. "Yeah, technically, but just to get us both in the same town. Everything else was you and me. I asked you out on a date, you agreed, we had a great time. Angela and Heather couldn't have planned that. They couldn't have manipulated the way we feel when we're together."

He was making a good point, but Liza still wasn't sure.

"You said it was fate, but that isn't fate."

Ben tentatively took a step forward and then another. When he was sure Liza wouldn't bolt away from him, he crossed the room and grabbed her hands in his. "Liza, as far as I'm concerned, you and I will always be fated. Whether it's all coincidence or planned out by someone else, I don't care. Fate, to me, is just about where you end up. We get to pick the way we get there, but the end result is fated, and no one will ever convince me otherwise."

Tears burned at the back of Liza's eyes, and she looked away from Ben, trying to regain control of her emotions.

That's when she caught sight of the campfire stove again and the s'mores ingredients scattered next to it on the floor.

"What's that for?"

Ben looked over his shoulder and smiled. "Oh, that. It's all I could find on short notice. When this place is a real kitchen, you'll have something a lot nicer, I'm sure."

Liza snapped her attention to him. "A real kitchen?"

He nodded. "This is going to be your Willow Beach headquarters."

She blinked. "You rented this place?"

"No, they did." Ben tipped his head towards the door, and Liza turned around just as Georgia, Stella, and Angela came inside.

They were all smiling, though Angela seemed nervous. Her hands were folded behind her back, and she was chewing on her lower lip.

"I don't know what's happening," Liza said, her throat feeling suddenly tight.

"I know you'd already decided to stay here in Willow Beach, but we wanted you to know how much we want you to stay," Stella said.

"And we wanted you to have an actual working kitchen," Georgia laughed. "I liked having you at the inn, of course, but it can't be a permanent solution."

Angela stepped forward, her eyes shifting between the floor and Liza's eyes. "And I wanted to say sorry for...everything."

"By buying me a kitchen space?" Liza shook her head. "It's too much. I can't ask you all to do that."

"You don't have to," Stella said. "Besides, we didn't buy it."

"We only paid rent for six months," Georgia said. "Willow Beach has a grant for new businesses that we signed you up for, and we got donations from a lot of people in town, too."

Liza's vision was blurry, and she swiped at her eyes, probably smearing makeup across her cheek. "You all did that for me?"

"For you and for the food," Georgia joked. "I assume you will be repaying us in the form of many free meals."

Everyone laughed, and Liza spun around, taking in the space. "I can't believe it."

"I know I may have ruined things for you a bit," Angela said, moving forward slowly. "But I really do think this town is the right fit for you, Aunt Liza. You seem so happy here, and I only want what is best for you. I shouldn't have gone about it the way I did, but—"

Liza pulled her niece in for a hug and kissed the top of her head. "It's okay. I forgive you."

They hugged for a minute before Stella cleared her throat. "I actually do have to get back to my gallery, though. My show is about to start."

"And we need to leave these two alone," Georgia said, holding out a hand to Angela. "Come on, dear. Let's walk over together."

Just as fast as they appeared, the three women left, and Liza and Ben were alone again.

Liza felt warmth along her back as Ben drew close to her. He wrapped his arms around her and rested his chin on the top of her head. "Do you like it?"

Liza spun around and looked up into his green eyes. "It's perfect. I love it here."

"I do, too," Ben said. "I've never felt the urge to settle down before, but suddenly, it sounds nice. I think that's because of you."

"I hope not *just* because of me?"

"No, not just," he admitted. "It's also because of this town, and the people in it. They are kind and generous. I mean, look at what they did for you." Ben gestured around at the storefront. "They care about people, and I want that in my life. I also want you in my life," he added. "If you'll have me."

Liza bit back a smile. "Make me a s'more, and we'll see how it goes."

The s'more was a mess—too much chocolate and marshmallow for the graham crackers to hold—but it didn't matter. Liza laughed when Ben got a string of melted marshmallow stuck on his nose, and he wiped chocolate off her upper lip. It was a mess, but wasn't everything?

When they finished their s'mores, Ben pulled out his phone and played the Chicago song that seemed to belong to the two of them in some way. He pulled her into his arms and they danced. Liza laid her head against Ben's chest, and after the tumultuousness of the last twenty-four hours, it felt like a dream.

It felt like fate.

EPILOGUE

One Month Later

"I can't believe Mrs. Albertson is never coming back," Sam said, shaking his head as he sliced into the roast beef Liza had just set in the middle of the long table.

"I know," Georgia said, echoing his shock. "She has lived in Willow Beach her entire life. Her dad used to run an apothecary."

"An apothecary?" Heather asked, one dark eyebrow raised. She looked so much like her dad it was jarring. "What is that?"

"An old-timey pharmacy," Ben answered, passing a bowl of mashed potatoes to Stella.

"What did she say?" Stella asked, drawing all eyes back to Liza. "In the email?"

Liza had received the email the day before. She'd been waiting for weeks to hear back from Mrs. Albertson in regards to her first request to extend her stay as a house sitter. She never expected Mrs. Albertson's counteroffer.

"She said she wanted to stay in the Philippines, and that I could have the cottage. Apparently, it belonged to her parents. It has been paid off for decades, and she doesn't want to worry about selling it."

Everyone seemed shocked she didn't even want money for it, but from what Liza could tell, Mrs. Albertson was pretty well off. During an especially vigorous spider hunt Liza had gone on after seeing the world's biggest spider crawl into her closet, Liza had found a few of Mrs. Albertson's bank statements. Usually, she wouldn't dare invade someone else's privacy like that, but there were so many zeroes it was hard not to take notice. Whatever the cottage was worth, it was nothing compared to what Mrs. Albertson had in her bank accounts.

Liza shrugged. "I didn't ask too many questions, honestly. She told me I could have an entire house for the cost of changing the title, so I accepted it."

"Smart," Heather said, tapping her temple with one finger. "Very smart."

Heather was in Willow Beach to see her dad for Thanksgiving, and Liza had really enjoyed getting to know her. Heather had apologized for her role in setting Liza and Ben up, but as far as Liza was concerned, all had been forgotten and forgiven. Liza didn't love the methods the two girls had used, but she was pleased enough with the results that she could let it go.

Liza had the cottage, Ben had a rental house close to the inn, and her kitchen space on Main Street was almost ready for business. At the very least, it was finished enough that she could host a lot of her friends there for Thanksgiving dinner. Alma was in Texas visiting family, and Cheri, Pam, and Barb were on a couples cruise with their husbands, but everyone else had been able to make it.

"Thanks for making all of the food," Katie said, holding up a caramelized brussel sprout on the end of her fork and pretending to kiss it. "This is so good that I might not save room for dessert."

"Blasphemy!" Stella shouted. "The turkey cupcakes you brought are divine, and everyone should eat one. I know because I already did."

"I also had one while I was helping out in the kitchen," Ben admitted sheepishly. "And I can confirm they are delicious."

"By 'helping,' he means taste-testing," Joel joked.

Liza and the book club ladies had all become close in the last month, and Ben had also connected with all of their significant others. In all her years in Boston, Liza had never had a large friend group, so she relished in it now. They got together regularly for pot luck meals and beach trips—which involved a lot of blankets and fires this time of year—and movie nights. It felt like a small, chosen family.

Dora was so jealous of Liza's large group of friends that she'd stopped telling Liza that she should move to California and, instead, was wondering if she should move back east.

"I hate the cold, but I love drinking with a large group of friends," Dora said. "It's a tough decision."

Liza knew Dora would never leave California, and part of her was glad. Dora gave Liza a reason to head to the land of sunshine—and a place to sleep when she got there. In fact, Liza and Ben already had a trip planned for February. Dora was anxious to see Ben after so long.

Once everyone was done eating, despite their groans of being too full to even look at food, they all had one of Katie's cupcakes. As Stella and Ben had said, they were incredible. Hazelnut cupcakes with salted caramel frosting and small candied turkeys stuck in the top.

As Liza was wiping frosting off her chin, Georgia stood up. "Well, everyone, this was a top-notch Thanksgiving get-together, but I'm afraid we have to get going."

"What about our gift exchange?" Joel asked.

Georgia turned to her boyfriend, face screwed up in confusion. "What gift exchange? It's Thanksgiving. You're a month ahead of schedule, buster."

Then, she saw him, and her mouth fell open.

Joel was down on one knee behind her, a black velvet ring box open in his palm.

"I just wanted to get you a little something," he said, his voice watery with unshed tears.

Georgia looked around the room, clearly in shock, and then her eyes found Joel again. They were like magnets, drawn together despite the murmur of excitement going through the room.

"Georgia Baldwin, you are the greatest woman I've ever known. Every day I spent not married to you is a tragedy. Will you marry me?"

Joel's proposal was simple and to the point—perfect for Georgia.

If Liza had learned anything about Georgia in the last two months, it was that Georgia knew what she wanted.

It was clear by the happy tears streaming down her face that she wanted this, too. She threw her arms around Joel's neck, nearly knocking him backward. "Yes. Yes, of course."

Everyone cheered, and Joel slipped the ring on Georgia's finger. She held it up to everyone, beaming from ear to ear...and then her smile wobbled.

"What is it?" Joel whispered in her ear.

She turned to him and said something Liza couldn't hear. At that, a smug smile crossed Joel's face, and he tipped his head towards the front door. Everyone looked in that direction.

Standing in the doorway were Georgia's three children, Drew, Tasha, and Melanie, who had tears streaming down her face.

"Get it together, Mel," Tasha teased, wiping at her own cheeks.

Georgia's smile returned full force, and she pulled her kids in for a hug. It was a precious moment for everyone to witness.

Hugs and congratulations were shared, and Georgia pulled Liza aside before the evening was over.

"You're staying in Willow Beach for the long haul, right?" she asked.

"Of course! This kitchen will be up and running in another week, and I'll be ready to book new appointments."

Georgia elbowed her. "That's good to hear because I may have a wedding you can cater soon."

Liza clapped and jumped once in excitement. "I would be absolutely honored. I will start planning a menu immediately. This is going to be so fun. We'll have so many taste-testing sessions you'll be sick of my cooking."

"I don't think that's possible," Georgia laughed.

All of a sudden, Katie appeared behind Georgia and cleared her throat pointedly.

"Relax, Katie. Of course, you're going to make my cake."

Katie wrapped her arms around Georgia's neck, and the two women mixed back in with the crowd.

Liza stood back, though, watching her friends.

Three years ago, she was finalizing her divorce, and even though Liza never would have admitted it, it felt like her life was over.

She couldn't imagine herself dating again or meeting new people. It didn't seem possible.

Even two months ago, she never imagined Willow Beach and the people who lived there would mean so much to her. She certainly never imagined she'd be moving there, expanding her business, and dating the love of her life.

Warm, familiar arms wrapped around Liza's waist, and she tipped her head back and kissed Ben's cheek.

"What are you thinking?" he whispered. "You have your thinking face on."

"I was thinking you're the love of my life."

He chuckled. "Liar."

Liza turned in his arms and rested her hands on his chest. "I'm serious. That's exactly what I was thinking. You are the love of my life, and I'm lucky to have so many amazing people in my life."

The smile that spread across Ben's face was luminous. Liza loved the laugh lines around his mouth and the wrinkles that fanned out from the corners of his eyes. She loved that she got the chance to see what this man looked like grown up. That even though she hadn't been there for every part of his life, she'd be there for the rest.

Gratitude overwhelmed her like a rogue wave, and she had to fight back tears as she looked into Ben's bright green eyes.

He bent down and pressed his lips to hers, cupping the back of her neck and tilting her back to deepen the kiss. It made her legs turn to jelly, and when he stood her back up, she clung to him for support.

"We are all lucky to have you," Ben said, pressing his forehead against hers. "Me most of all."

Someone shouted behind her, drawing everyone's attention. Stella had knocked over a bottle of wine, and it was soaking into the tablecloth and dripping on the floor. Stella, Georgia, and Katie all turned to grab a towel and ran into one another, sending Georgia sprawling onto her butt. Joel laughed, Georgia threatened not to marry him if he didn't help her up, and Ben wrapped his arm around

Liza's shoulders so they could watch the whole event unfold from the corner of the room.

Things rarely went to plan in life, but with the right people and the right attitude, Liza had learned everything could still turn out perfectly.

∾

Thanks for reading JUST SOUTH OF SUNRISE! If you loved the Baldwin family and Willow Beach, you'll fall head over heels for the Benson family in my beloved Sweet Island Inn series, set on the gorgeous island of Nantucket. Take a sneak preview below of Book 1 in the series, NO HOME LIKE NANTUCKET.

∾

NO HOME LIKE NANTUCKET:
A Sweet Island Inn Novel (Book 1)

Nantucket was their paradise—until reality came barging in.

An unexpected pregnancy.

A marriage on the rocks.

A forbidden workplace romance.

And a tragedy no one could have seen coming.

Take a trip to Nantucket's Sweet Island Inn and follow along as Mae Benson and her children—the Wall Street queen Eliza, stay-at-home mom Holly, headstrong chef Sara, and happy-go-lucky fisherman Brent—face the hardest summer of their lives.

Love, loss, heartbreak, hope—it's all here and more. Can the Benson family find a way to forgive themselves and each other? Or will their grief be too much to overcome?

Find out in **NO HOME LIKE NANTUCKET.**

Click here to start reading now!

∼

Chapter One: Mae

Mae Benson never ever slept in.

For each of the one thousand, two hundred, and eleven days that she'd lived at 114 Howard Street, Nantucket, Massachusetts, she'd gotten up with the dawn and started her morning the second her eyes opened. It wasn't because she was a busybody, or compulsive, or obsessive. On the contrary, snoozing for a while was tempting. Her bed was soft this morning. The first fingers of springtime sunlight had barely begun to peek in through the gauzy curtains that hung over the window. And she was in that perfect sleeping position— warm but not too warm, wrapped up but not too tightly.

But force of habit could sometimes be awfully hard to break. So, being careful to make as little noise as possible, she slid out from underneath the comforter, tucked her feet into the fuzzy slippers she'd received for her sixtieth birthday last year, and rose.

Her husband, Henry, always called her his little hummingbird. He'd even bought her a beautiful handblown hummingbird ornament for Christmas last year from a glassblower down by the wharf. It had jade-green wings, little amethysts for eyes, and a patch of ruby red on its chest. She loved how it caught and refracted the winter sunbeams, and she always made sure to put it on a limb of the tree where it could see the snow falling outdoors.

"Flitting around the house, are we?" Henry would say, laughing, every time he came downstairs from their master bedroom to find Mae buzzing from corner to corner. She would just laugh and shake her head. He could make fun of her all he wanted, but the fact remained that each of the little projects she had running at all times around the house required love and care from the moment the day began.

She ran through the list in her head as she moved silently around the bedroom getting dressed for the day. She needed to water the plants on the living room windowsill, the ones that her daughter, Sara, had sent from her culinary trip to Africa and made her mother promise to keep alive until she could retrieve them on her next visit. Crane flowers, with their gorgeous mix of orange- and blue-bladed leaves; desert roses, with their soft blush of red fading into the purest white; and her favorites, the fire lilies, that looked just like a flickering flame.

She had to check on the batch of marshmallow fluff fudge—a Mae Benson specialty—that she'd left to set in the freezer overnight. Her friend Lola, who lived down the street, had just twisted her ankle badly a few days prior and was laid up at home with a boot on her leg. Mae didn't know much about ankle injuries, but she had a lot of hands-on experience with fudge, so she figured she'd offer what she knew best.

She should also start coffee for Henry—lots of cream and sugar, as always. Henry had an outing planned that morning with Brent to go check on some fishing spots they'd been scheming over for the last few weeks. Mae knew he was excited about the trip. He'd been exhibiting trademark Happy Henry behavior all week long—eyes lighting up with that mischievous twinkle, hands rubbing together like an evil mastermind, and the way that he licked the corner of his lips, like he could already taste the salt air that hung on the wind and feel the bouncing of the boat as it raced through the waves.

Just before she turned to leave the bedroom and start her day, she looked over at her husband. He was sleeping on his side of the bed, snoring softly like he always did. It was never enough to wake her, thankfully. Not like Lola's ex-husband, who'd been a snorer of epic proportions. Henry hadn't bothered a single soul in the six and a half decades he'd been alive on this earth. Matter of fact, she couldn't think of a single person who disliked him—other than Mae herself, whenever he took the liberty of dipping into the brownie batter, or when he insisted on sneaking up behind her while she was cooking, nipping at the lobe of her ear, then dancing away and laughing when she tried to swat him with a spoon and inevitably sprayed chocolate batter all over the kitchen.

But the truth of the matter was that she could never bring herself to stay irked at him. It wasn't just his physical looks, although he certainly wasn't hurting in that department. The same things she'd fallen in love with at that Boston bar forty-plus years ago were still present and accounted for. The long, proud nose. Full lips, always eager to twitch into a smile. Bright blue eyes that danced in the sunlight when he laughed, cried, and—well, all the time, really. And that darn shock of hair that was perpetually threatening to fall over his forehead. She reached over and smoothed it out of his face now. Time had turned his sun-drenched blondness into something more silvery, but in Mae's eyes, he was all the more handsome for it.

But, even more than his good looks, Mae loved Henry's soul. He was a selfless giver, an instant friend to every child who'd ever come across his path. He loved nothing more than to kneel in front of an awestruck five-year-old and present him or her with some little hand-carved trinket, one of the many he kept in his pockets to whittle whenever he had an idle moment. She loved that he laughed and cried in all the wrong places during romantic comedies and that he knew how to cook—how to *really* cook, the kind of cooking you do with a jazz record crooning through the speakers and a soft breeze drifting in through an open window.

She let her hand linger on Henry's forehead just a beat too long. He didn't open his eyes, but his hand snaked up from underneath the sheets and threaded through Mae's fingers.

"You're getting up?"

"Can't waste the day away."

It was a ritual, one they'd been through practically every morning for as long as either could remember. For all that he'd become a proud father to four children, a state-record-holding fisherman, a much-sought-after contractor and builder on the island of Nantucket, Henry loved nothing so much as to stay in bed for hours, alternating between sleeping and poking Mae until she rolled over and gave him the soft kisses he called her "hummingbird pecks." There was a perpetual little boy spirit in him, a playfulness that another six or sixty decades couldn't extinguish if it tried.

"Stay with me," he murmured. "The day can wait a few more minutes, can't it?" His eyes were open now, heavy with sleep, but still gazing at her fondly.

Mae tapped him playfully on the tip of the nose. "If it was up to you, 'a few more minutes' would turn into hours before we knew it, and then I'd be scrambling around like a chicken with my head cut off, trying to get everything done before Holly, Pete, and the kids get here tonight."

Holly was Mae and Henry's middle daughter. She and her husband, Pete, were bringing their two kids to Nantucket to spend the weekend. Mae had had the date circled on her calendar for months, excited at the prospect of spoiling her grandkids rotten. She already had oodles of activities planned—walks downtown to get rock candy from the corner store, sandcastles at the beach, bike rides down to 'Sconset to ogle the grand houses the rich folks had built out on that end of the island.

Grady was a little wrecking ball of a seven-year-old boy, and Mae knew that he'd love nothing so much as building a massive sandcastle and then terrorizing it like a blond Godzilla. Alice, on the other hand, was still as sweet and loving as a five-year-old girl could be. She let Grandma Mae braid her long, soft hair into fishtails every morning whenever they were visiting the island. It was another ritual that Mae treasured beyond anything else. Her life was full of those kinds of moments.

"It ain't so bad, lying in bed with me, is it?" Henry teased. "But maybe I just won't give ya a choice!"

He leaped up and threw his arms around Mae's waist, tugging her over him and then dragging them both beneath the covers. Mae yelped in surprise and smacked him on the chest, but Henry was a big man—nearly six and a half feet tall—and the years he'd spent hauling in fish during his weekend trips with Brent had kept him muscular and toned. When her palm landed on his shoulder, it just made a thwacking noise, and did about as much good as if she'd slapped a brick wall. So she just laughed and let Henry pull her into his arms, roll over on top of her, and throw the comforter over their heads.

It was soft and warm and white underneath. The April sun filtered through the bedsheets and cast everything in a beautiful, hazy glow. "You've never looked so beautiful," Henry said, his face suspended above hers.

"Henry Benson, I do believe you are yanking my chain," she admonished.

"Never," he said, and he said it with such utter seriousness that Mae's retort fell from her lips. Instead of poking him in the chest like she always did whenever he teased her, she let her hand stroke the line of his jaw.

He pressed a gentle kiss to her lips. "Stay with me for just a few more minutes, Mrs. Benson," he said. She could feel him smiling as he kissed her. She could also feel the butterflies fluttering in her stomach. Forty-one years of marriage and four children later, and she still got butterflies when her husband kissed her. Wasn't that something?

"All right, Mr. Benson," she said, letting her head fall back on the pillows. "Just a few more minutes."

Henry grinned and fell in next to her, pulling her into his embrace. She could feel his heartbeat thumping in his chest. Familiar. Dependent. Reliable. Hers. "You just made my day."

"But I'm warning you," she continued, raising one finger into the air and biting back the smile that wanted to steal over her lips. "If you start snoring again, I'm smothering you with a pillow."

"Warning received," Henry said. "Now quit making a fuss and snooze with me for a while, darling."

So Mae did exactly that. Sara's plants could wait.

Click here to keep reading!

ALSO BY GRACE PALMER

Sweet Island Inn

No Home Like Nantucket (Book 1)

No Beach Like Nantucket (Book 2)

No Wedding Like Nantucket (Book 3)

No Love Like Nantucket (Book 4)

Willow Beach Inn

Just South of Paradise (Book 1)

Just South of Perfect (Book 2)

Just South of Sunrise (Book 3)

Made in United States
North Haven, CT
07 July 2022